Pierre Lemaitre

ROSY & JOHN

Translated from the French by
Frank Wynne

MACLEHOSE PRESS
QUERCUS · LONDON

First published in the French language as *Rosy & John* by La Librairie Générale
Française in 2013
First published in Great Britain in 2017 by MacLehose Press
This paperback edition published in 2021 by

MacLehose Press
an imprint of Quercus Publishing Ltd
Carmelite House
50 Victoria Embankment
London EC4Y 0DZ

Published by special arrangement with La Librairie Générale Française and
its duly appointed agency, 2 Seas Literary Agency

A CIP catalogue record for this book is available from the British Library.

ISBN (MMP) 978 1 529416 800
ISBN (Ebook) 978 1 84866 601 6

10 9 8 7 6 5 4 3 2 1

Designed and typeset in Minion by Libanus Press Ltd
Printed and bound in Great Britain by Clays Ltd, Elcograf S.p.A.

MIX
Paper from
responsible sources
FSC® C104740

For Pascaline

For Dominique and Jean-Paul Vormus
with my friendship.

"There are cases (rather rare, it is true) where the best way to gain time is to change place."

MARCEL PROUST, *À l'ombre des jeunes filles en fleurs*

DAY ONE

DAY ONE

5.00 p.m.
The unexpected encounter that will forever change your life, the treacherous patch of black ice, the answer you give without thinking . . . It takes only a split second for such decisive events to occur.

Take this little boy, for example, he is eight years old. He has only to make one false step and his whole world might change irreversibly. His mother once had a tarot reading where she was told she would be widowed within the year. She shared this information with her son, her lower lip quivering, her hands clawing at her chest, her voice tremulous with sobs. I had to tell someone, you do understand, don't you? The little boy had never imagined the death of his father, who seemed to him immortal. Now, he lives in constant fear. Some mothers, honestly . . . This particular mother is thirty but has all the maturity of a teenage schoolgirl. She has long since forgotten this prediction (besides her thoughtlessness, she is also quite scatter-brained, one thought displaces the previous at a frantic rate). For her young son, however, it is a very different matter. His imagination has been overwhelmed by this witch's tale, he dares not talk to anyone about it; he has constant nightmares. There are days when he is so consumed by the idea of his father's death it makes him ill; then, for weeks at a time, it will disappear, as if by magic. When it returns, it is with a savage ferocity that makes his knees buckle, forcing him to cling to something, to sit down.

When the threat resurfaces, he resorts to all kinds of rituals, convinced that if his father dies, it will be his fault.

Today: "If I don't step on a crack, my father won't die." It only counts after he passes the boulangerie.

He has scarcely been able to breathe since he left the house, and there is a long way still to go before he reaches his music lesson. Something tells him that this time he will not make it, but he can think of nothing, no excuse that would allow him to give up his challenge. One street, two streets, already he can see the boulevard, but the panic is rising and it seems to him that the closer he comes to deliverance, the closer he comes to catastrophe. He stares at the pavement as he walks, his clarinet case dangling from his wrist. He is sweating. He is two hundred metres from the music school. For no apparent reason – a sense of foreboding perhaps – he looks up and suddenly he sees his father coming in the other direction. There is scaffolding here that forces his father to make a detour, along a wooden walkway that juts out into the street. It is very narrow. Shoulders hunched, his father is walking quickly, decisively. When he walks like this, he looks as though nothing could stop him. The boy is surprised because it is unusual to see him coming home so early.

The slow-motion images that follow will forever be

engraved on his memory. Needless to say, this momentary lapse of concentration is all it takes. When he realises his mistake and looks back down at the pavement, he stops dead: his foot is squarely planted on a crack between the paving stones . . .

His father is going to die, it is inevitable.

It takes only a split second for decisive events to occur.

Take the young woman who is walking a little way behind this boy. Not particularly pretty, an economics student, she has never had sex. "The opportunity never presented itself," she says simply. The truth is more complicated, but that does not matter. It is May, she is twenty-two years old, and all that matters is that at this precise moment she has arrived at the corner of rue Joseph-Merlin, where she now waits for a man who wants her: this is why he suggested that they meet, to tell her that he desires her. She has only to say yes or no and everything will change one way or the other. Nor will it simply affect the pedestrian matter of her virginity. Because she will say no. The man will say that he understands (yeah, right) . . . she will watch him walk away, and just as she is beginning to regret her decision and wants to call him back . . .

Too late.

The explosion is so powerful it rocks the whole neighbourhood. It is like an earthquake, the shockwaves are felt a hundred metres away.

In a split second, the little boy sees the body of his father soar into the air as though a giant hand has punched him in the solar plexus. The young woman scarcely has time to open her mouth when her ex-future lover is swept off his feet and thrown through the glass shop front of Women's Secret.

The rue Joseph-Merlin is a shopping precinct. Clothes shops, shoe shops, delicatessens, dry cleaners, pharmacies . . . it is the most commercial street in the area. To find anything better would mean walking as far as the junction with avenue Pradelle. It is May 20: for days now, a warm summer sun has settled over the city. At 5 p.m., it feels almost like a July afternoon with its tempting promise of an aperitif on a café terrace, there are people everywhere, so, naturally, when the bomb explodes, it is a tragedy, but it is also an injustice.

Then again, if there were any justice in this world . . .

Pedestrians thrown to the ground shield themselves with their arms. A woman in a print dress is pitched backwards, her head slamming against the wooden posts in front of the scaffolding. On the far side of the street, a man dismounting from his moped is hit by an iron bar that appears from nowhere, it shatters his pelvis, doubling him in two; although he is still wearing his crash helmet, it may not be enough to save his life.

The roar of the explosion is followed by an ear-splitting shriek of metal: having wavered briefly after the blast, as though taking a moment to think, the huge edifice of scaffolding shudders, lifts slightly off the ground, and crumples, as though slumping onto the pavement, like those tower blocks dynamited on television that seem to dissolve in an instant. On the pavement opposite, a girl in high-heeled white boots looks up and sees the scaffolding poles disperse like sparks from a firework and fall towards her in a rain as slow as it is inexorable ...

The explosion obliterates shop windows, cars, the very thoughts in people's heads. In these endless seconds, no-one can think, ideas seem to have been snuffed out like candles. Even ordinary sounds have been obliterated, a tremulous, unsettling silence hangs over the scene, as though every last person in the city has been killed outright.

When finally the reality of the situation gathers momentum, it flares into every mind. Above the street, those windows not shattered by the explosion timidly begin to open and incredulous faces appear.

Down below, the survivors struggle to their feet and stare, uncomprehending, at the new cityscape.

A war-torn city.

Shop fronts have vanished, the walls behind the scaffolding have collapsed, sending up clouds of plaster dust that settles slowly like tainted snow. The most spectacular new landmark is the vast pile of metal poles and planks that all but blocks the street, four storeys of scaffolding make for an impressive heap. The collapse was almost vertically, completely crushing two parked cars. The heap of planks bristling with metal rods pointing towards the heavens looks like a giant mohawk.

How many are buried beneath the rubble, the shards of glass, the slabs of tarmac? It is impossible to say.

Here and there lie a few prone bodies, a scattering of

soil and sand and settling dust, but there are strange sights, like the blue-trimmed jacket on the coat hanger dangling from a "No Entry" sign. The sort of things one might see in houses ravaged by an earthquake: a baby's cot, a doll, a bride's tiara, small objects that God seems to have carefully placed here and there to illustrate the black irony of His mysterious ways.

Before his son's astonished eyes, the father traced an improbable arc. The explosion that lifted him off the wooden walkway has set him down on the bonnet of a parked van where he sits, motionless, looking for all the world as though he is about to play a game of dominoes with his son, but his eyes are vacant, his face blood-streaked, his head lists to left and right as though trying to ease a crick in his neck.

The little boy was also swept up by the explosion. His eyes wide, one cheek pressed against the pavement, he is lying next to the portico that broke his flight, still clutching the clarinet case that has snapped open; the clarinet is gone, it will never be found.

Sirens begin to wail.

Confusion gives way to a sense of urgency, a rush of energy, of compassion; those who survived unscathed race towards the fallen bodies.

Some struggle to their feet only to fall to their knees, exhausted.

The dazed silence is followed by a growing clamour of shouts, screams, orders, whistles.

Whimpers are drowned out by a chorus of car horns.

5.01 p.m.

The man on the corner of the rue Joseph-Merlin and rue Général-Morieux has missed nothing. Although he is almost thirty, most people would call him a boy, there is something childlike about him, something immature that contrasts sharply with his heavyset, farmhand's build. He may be self-conscious, but he is anything but inept. In fact, he built the bomb himself . . . He set it to go off at 5 p.m., but that was more in hope than expectation – it's impossible to tell if these things are going to work properly.

Or even if they will work at all.

His anxiety is easier to understand when one knows that this is his first bomb. Several weeks' work. He had no real sense of the damage it would cause. Despite his damage assessments, this was the one unknown factor. A professional would doubtless be able to make predictions with a greater degree of certainty. This man is an amateur, forced for the most part to rely on instinct. He did all the necessary theoretical calculations, but everyone knows that life and theory are two very different things. But he did the best he could with the means at his disposal. After that, as Rosie always says, "Work won't get you everything in this life. You also need a little luck."

The young man gets up from his terrace table and leaves without paying – not that anyone will notice this. In a few quick strides, he is far away, heading towards the métro.

Let's call him Jean. In fact, his name is John, but that is

a long story. Since his teens he has been calling himself Jean, something we will come back to later. But, for the moment, Jean.

The bomb worked pretty well; on that score, he has every reason to be pleased. Though he has concerns about the eventual death toll, it should bear fruit.

The walking wounded are already hurrying to help those still sprawled in the street. Jean disappears into the métro station.

He will help no-one. It was he who planted the bomb.

5.10 p.m.
Camille Verhœven is four feet eleven of towering rage. Four feet eleven may not be much in a man, but in terms of concentrated fury it is colossal. Especially as, in a cop, rage, even when supressed, is not a cardinal virtue. At most, it is a boon to journalists (in various media appearances, his razor-sharp comments have made for blistering copy), but more generally, it is a headache for his superiors, for witnesses, colleagues, prosecutors – pretty much everybody.

Camille has been known to rant, to lose his temper on rare occasions, but he is careful to watch his step. His is the type to seethe rather than lash out and punch the nearest object. Which is just as well since, given his stature, the controls in his car are mounted on the steering wheel so a driver needs to be careful: one false move and you'll find yourself in a ditch.

The reason for today's fury (he finds a new one

every day) came to him while he was shaving, he caught a glimpse of himself in the mirror and did not like what he saw. He has never much liked the way he looks, but for many years he successfully suppressed the bitterness he feels at not having grown up like everyone else. But since the death of his wife, Irène, there have been moments when his self-loathing has seemed frankly alarming.

It has been six months since he took a day off. His last major case ended in failure: the girl he was tracking was dead by the time he found her,[1] it had left him quite shaken up. (In truth, it was not a total failure, he successfully arrested a killer, but to Camille the glass is always half-empty.) So he took a couple of days. He almost suggested to Anne that she come down to the country for a day or two, it was a perfect opportunity to show her his bolthole, but they had not known each other for long, and he decided he would rather be on his own.

He spent three days sketching, painting. He has too much talent to be a cop, not enough to be an artist. So he became a cop. Besides, he never wanted to be an artist.

Camille never listens to music while driving, any more than he does at home: he finds it distracting. With his laconic turn of phrase, he simplifies things by saying "I don't like music". And, deep down, this is true, if he liked music he would buy it, listen to it. But he never does. For those around him – *what? how can you not like music?* – this is unimaginable, they cannot believe it, they quiz him

1 *Alex*, MacLehose Press, 2013

about it, they stare at him, dumbfounded. Not liking art or literature, now that would be alright, that's understandable, but music? So Verhœven lays it on with a trowel, he can't help it, he finds their reaction infuriating – he can be a complete pain in the arse sometimes. Once Irène said to him "It's a pity you don't know more misogynists, you'd help them put things in perspective."

Since music is out of the question, Verhœven listens to talk radio non-stop.

The first newsflash comes just as he turns on the radio. ". . . *a powerful explosion in Paris' eighteenth arrondissement. The cause of the blast is not yet known, but the extent of the catastrophe is considerable.*"

The sort of news story you listen to only if you live in the area, or if the body count is truly spectacular.

Verhœven carries on driving, following the sequence of news bulletins: "*Emergency services are already at the scene. The number of victims has not been confirmed. According to witnesses, it would appear that . . .*"

Verhœven's only thought is that this will mean traffic jams as he approaches Paris.

5.20 p.m.

A first-world country is truly something.

Hardly have the victims had time to gather their thoughts than the firefighters are on the scene. Four stations mobilised. Ambulances and paramedics from S.A.M.U. are hurtling towards the scene, while just outside the cordon set up by the police, paramedic units are throwing open the doors of their vans and unloading stretchers, emergency foil blankets, I.V. drips, boxes filled with pharmaceutical supplies, antiseptics, bandages; quickly, professionally, the unruffled paramedics take up the positions assigned to them on the Emergency Evacuation Plan that has been drawn up. Paramedics are already at work. The *Securité civile* is organising and coordinating efforts, setting up lines of communication. The triage tents seem to mushroom out of the rain of dust that is still falling.

From this angle, it is easy to see where our taxes go.

And then there are the journalists. They are professionals too. Mobile broadcast units from radio and rolling T.V. news channels arrive with the emergency services: technicians unspool cables, make ready for the first live transmission; journalists are playing at war correspondents, scanning for an ideal spot, a place where the wreckage will be visible in the background as they deliver their report.

This is the meaning of modern democracy: a country where professionals have seized power.

5.30 p.m.

Ministère de l'Intérieur. Crisis meeting.

"What does the president say?" asks the private secretary.

The minister does not answer, what the president has to say is nobody's business. Especially since, like everyone else, *Monsieur le président* is waiting for more information.

The minister steps further into the room, but remains standing, a clear sign that he does not intend to be here long. With a nod, he gives the floor to the head of the General Directorate for Internal Security, who confirms what everyone has been thinking ever since news of the explosion broke: there were no Islamist terrorists involved. It may not last, but for now at least, things are calm on that score. Over the past months, steady progress has been made in top-secret talks with key cells and Islamist groups: though hotly denying it, the government is about to make a huge payment for the return of two hostages, so it would not be in the interest of the fundamentalists to cut the pipeline allowing them to hoover wads of cash from the Treasury. Besides which, nothing about the attack corresponds to their usual M.O. and choice of target, there have been no reports of suspicious behaviour either from informants or undercover agents, nothing, absolutely nothing . . .

"So, we're ruling out religious motives for the attack."

This leaves political motives. A much more complicated terrain. The intelligence services have had no new information in recent months, but the constellation of political factions and guerrilla groups is so vast . . . Such groups are born and die every day; they are unstable, constantly in transition, it is impossible to rule out a lone wolf attack.

"Right now, it's all hands on deck."

As for the death toll, initial estimates should come through in about an hour. Two hours, max.

The minister nods. He turns to the press secretary.

"As far as the media are concerned, investigations are ongoing. Nothing more."

He calmly surveys those present.

"And I don't want anyone doing anything until I give the word. Let me make myself absolutely clear: there is to be no precipitate action, no suspicious commotion in the ranks."

An unambiguous communiqué to the media: the government is not panicking.

Message received loud and clear.

A car is waiting downstairs, the minister is going to visit the site of the attack, to demonstrate his compassion, to reassure the public that *"intelligence services and law enforcement are committed to tracking down those responsible blah blah blah"*.

Tragedy is part of the job.

5.55 p.m.
The nannies and childminders gathered in the square Dupeyroux shift their chairs closer together to chat; near the adventure playground, a few fretful mothers watch their darlings' daring feats. Jean usually sits in the middle of the square. He has his own bench, after a fashion.

Brash but benevolent in his park keeper's uniform, Marcel reigns as lord and master here, though ever-ready with his whistle, in a career spanning twenty-four years he has never had to deal with an breach of the bylaws. Acquainted with the regulars, he nods to Jean as he passes.

He is a little like an attentive barman, his job security depends on his devotion to his clientele.

Jean is seated as he always is, back straight, knees together, clasped hands pressed between his thighs. As the keeper passes, he moves his lips almost imperceptibly, this is how he greets people. No-one has ever seen him with a newspaper or a mobile phone; he gazes at the square, engrossed in his thoughts. This afternoon, he sits in his usual spot, he is blinking nervously, his heart is still hammering, but on the surface, it is impossible to imagine that this boy has just detonated a bomb in the neighbouring arrondissement. Even from here, it is still possible to hear the wail of sirens and ambulances hurtling down the boulevard heading for the rue Joseph-Merlin.

The park keeper moves on, quick glance to left and right, Jean gets to his feet, ducks around the bench and dives into the bushes. On his hands and knees, hidden by the dense foliage, he uses the tool he fashioned to lift the steel hatch. The metal screeches, it is a tricky procedure, though the most difficult part, once he has slipped inside, is lowering the cover back into place without making any noise. A few days ago, when he transported the bomb and all his equipment here, it was a nightmare.

He is now hunkered inside a narrow concrete cubicle. This is the entrance to a "telecoms exchange". The impressive tangle of pipes and power lines and fibre optic cables that services the local neighbourhood snakes through here. Most of these substations are located under roads, beneath cast-iron manhole covers. There are hundreds of them in Paris, as there are in all the major cities throughout France. Jean stumbled on this one almost by accident while recovering a lost ball for a kid too scared to go into the thicket.

It takes a minute for him to calm himself, then he takes a torch from his jacket pocket and checks that the coast is clear, that no-one has been down here since his last visit.

The light illuminates a low-ceilinged corridor some fifteen metres long, where he has to crouch slightly in order to get through. At the far end, there is a large room where he can once again stand upright. The walls are lined with meters and junction boxes and two electrical control cabinets on which terse signs in red and black warn that the imprudent visitor will be summarily electrocuted. Signs that would make Jean laugh, if he were so disposed.

He takes off his jacket, folds it neatly, sets it on the floor and, sitting cross-legged, one by one he takes the tools from the backpack he leaves here between visits. Though this time he will take it away with him since he has no need to come back again. He turns off the torch, flicks on the headlamp he uses for precision tasks and sets to work.

He is at the very centre of the square Dupeyroux.

Above his head and a few metres to his right is the toddlers' playground with its slides and swings and spring riders, and a hill of cubes that serves as a climbing frame.

The kids love it.

As soon as he gets home and opens the door, Camille apologises to his tabby cat, Doudouche – a piece of work, just like her master – for abandoning her for three whole days. He throws open the windows and, while the cat perches on the table pretending to ignore him (she's a drama queen), he peels off his jacket, replenishes the kibble in her bowl and, for a treat, pours a little cold milk into a saucer and sets it on the floor.

"Doudouche?"

She is pointedly staring out the window.

"Well, it's right here," Camille says. "The rest is up to you."

Then as a treat for himself, he pours a little whisky.

He is dissatisfied with his enforced leave. Because he chose to spend it on his own? On the answering machine, there is a message from Anne. A warm voice: "If you don't get back too late, fancy coming round to mine for dinner?" It is strange, Camille had not wanted to take her to Montfort, yet in her absence he spent his whole time drawing her. As he sips his whisky, he leafs through the sketches. He always works from memory. Anything that strikes him in the everyday (faces, figures, expressions, quotidian details) eventually finds its way into his sketchpad.

He continues to flick through the drawings as he dials Anne's number.

"Depends what's for dinner," he says straight off.

"You're a complete boor, aren't you . . ."

At either end of the line, they both smile.

There follows a long, tremulous silence in which they say many things to each other.

"Be there in about an hour, O.K.?"

6.05 p.m.

An hour after the explosion, all the wounded from the rue Joseph-Merlin have been evacuated by the emergency services.

Right now, the toll seems nothing short of a miracle: twenty-eight injured, no fatalities. "At least not yet," say the pessimists, but there are no patients in a critical condition. Broken arms and legs, dislocations, contusions, bruises, fractures, burns, cracked ribs, these things will require surgery and weeks of physiotherapy, but the real damage has been to the mind, not the body. The little boy escaped with a broken arm; at school, the kids will think he is a hero, his classmates will line up to sign his cast. The young virgin found herself on her backside; her beau, for his part, was taken to A&E with a dislocated shoulder and will have to explain to his wife how he came to be found flat on his back in a lingerie shop in a neighbourhood where he had no business being.

Of course, it is still possible that a body might be found under the rubble (under the heap of scaffolding poles, for example), but the whole area has been scanned by experts, sniffer dogs have done their work. Verdict: no bodies under the rubble.

A miracle.

The reporters are quick to pick up on the word and run with it. These are seasoned professionals, give them a non-story and they'll turn it into a major news item. In this case, they go for the miraculous reprieve. O.K., so a few deaths would have played better, easy to manage, guaranteed results. With the living, you have to put in more effort, but it's just a matter of experience. Experience is what marks them out as professionals. There is no shortage of police officers at the scene. At least thirty of them, primed and ready for action, some from the anti-terrorist squad. Some of them – with the approval of the paramedics – have managed to question victims with minor injuries before they were evacuated, but most of them are patrolling the neighbourhood looking for external witnesses, residents with windows overlooking the crime scene, shopkeepers, passers-by who were not directly affected by the explosion.

They are in constant contact with teams back at the station who are busy looking up the names of landlords, tenants, shop owners, checking databases, reviewing C.C.T.V. footage from two nearby cameras (though it seems likely they will have captured nothing of interest, given their position and their angle); as soon as they succeed in identifying a witness or a passer-by, they scan any and every relevant file – barely an hour after the attack took place, terabytes of data have already been scrutinised.

And, right now, the only reliable witness statement is that given by Clémence Kriszewckanszki.

Her name is so difficult to spell that people always

make the effort . . . In her twenty-two years, she has seen it misspelled only twice. Physically, she is unremarkable, the sort of woman who scarcely gets a second glance. She was the young woman sitting on the café terrace a few metres from Jean. When the bomb exploded, the young man with her was thrown backwards and cracked his skull, he has been taken to hospital.

"Julien . . ." she says, her voice almost a whisper.

"Julien what?" asks the officer, pen at the ready.

She is embarrassed, there they were kissing, cuddling, but she does not know his surname. A friend of a friend . . . She puckers her lips, she is terrified of seeming like a slut. But as far as the cop is concerned she could have been on the game since the age of thirteen for all he cares, it is the least of his worries: she may have seen the bomber, that is all that matters.

There are three of them clustered around her, sitting on red plastic chairs in the back room of a restaurant whose windows were shattered by the explosion.

"Tall," Clémence remembers. "One metre eighty or a little more. There was something awkward about him, you know what I mean? Clumsy. Dark brown hair falling over his forehead, a small liver spot under his right eye, thick lips, he was wearing a pair of beige jeans with bright stitching and a belt with a Harley Davidson buckle. He . . ."

"Hold up, hold up," the cop interrupts, visibly overwhelmed. "You noticed his belt buckle?"

Without waiting for her to reply, the commander

whispers something to the third officer who immediately gets up and leaves the room.

The cops are sceptical. Clémence looks at them, puzzled. The commander nods, carry on. She continues her statement, detailing the clothes worn by the young man, the make of his mobile phone, the bag he set down next to him, his shoes, even his gestures, and especially the way he balanced his phone on the table in front of him, training the camera at the building . . . A young plain-clothes officer bursts in, looking harried, puts a piece of paper on the table, mutters something and goes out again. The three men stare silently at Clémence.

She stares at each of them in turn, she does not understand what is going on.

"The officer who just came in," says the commander, "could you describe him?"

It is a classic ploy, but what else could they do?

"About thirty, I'd say." Clémence speaks as though she is stating the obvious, repeating something everyone already knows. "Blue trousers, flared at the ankles, a Jacquard-style jumper with a blue chevron design, a gold medal on a chain around his neck . . ."

The three officers exchange half-smiles; the judge is going to love this witness.

They go back to the description of the bomber. They summon an artist from *Identité judiciaire* to do an Identikit. A hyper-realistic portrait, even the kids who knew him in kindergarten would recognise him.

Things rarely get off to such a good start.

6.08 p.m.

Meanwhile, less than a hundred metres away, two men are about to shed a disconcerting light on the case.

The first is Basin, the head of the crime lab attached to the *Préfecture*. In his fifties, tall and broad-shouldered, he hails from the South West where he spent his youth playing rugby, but was never quite good enough to make it as a professional, he has the hands of a lacemaker. Ill-suited to a rugby ball, but perfect for a bomb disposal expert.

He is standing in front of the crater left by the explosion. He has seen a lot of things in his career, but this has him bewildered.

"Ah, shit," grumbles a voice nearby.

It is Forestier, a colleague, one of the old school, he lost a finger in Kosovo and has never been the same since. Under normal circumstances, losing a finger would not seem like the end of the world, but when you believe you're immortal, it is devastating. He is also staring into the hole. It is only partly visible through the pile of scaffolding poles, but for guys like these, a small part of the crater, a glimpse of the rim, is enough for them to reconstruct the whole crime scene.

And, when the scene has finally been cleared, this particular crater will measure three to four metres in circumference with a depth of more than a metre.

"Fucking hell," says Forestier.

Both men are flabbergasted.

They nod and exchange a wary smile, but this should not be seen as cynicism, it is purely professional.

Though it is true that it has been a long time since anyone saw a 140-mm mortar shell in the centre of Paris.

7.00 p.m.

"Jesus! A mortar shell?"

"Yes, *Monsieur le ministre*," says the expert from *Securité civile*. "Probably dating back to the First World War."

"And these things are still functional?"

"Not always, *Monsieur le ministre*, most of them are defective. But obviously the one on the rue Joseph-Merlin was in working order."

The minister turns to the officer from the D.G.S.I. and gives him a quizzical look. The civil servant pulls a face intended to convey his embarrassment.

"We are not dealing with a classic scenario here. If this is an isolated attack, we're looking for a needle in a haystack. We have to hope that some organisation will claim responsibility. And ideally demand a ransom. That way we'll have something to get our teeth into. In the meantime, we need to focus on gun collectors, freaks obsessed with the First World War, the handful of factions we consider capable of violence, comb through any recent threats that were overlooked. Scrape together whatever information we can. Blindly."

The minister is a man of action. He hates it when there is nothing to do but to wait.

He gets to his feet, he has to go and report to the president's office. This prospect is one he finds reassuring.

A minister's job is to deal with one clusterfuck a minute. The president has to deal with three.

7.15 p.m.

But for the traffic jams, Camille would have arrived at Anne's place on time. As a rule, he is punctual. But as though the constant stream of news flashes were not enough (". . . *the* ministre de l'Intérieur *is visiting the scene of the blast* . . ."), his route took him within an arrondissement of the rue Joseph-Merlin, a guaranteed catastrophe. As soon as he found himself in the middle of a gridlock, he realised he was screwed. He was not far from his destination in terms of distance, but in terms of time . . . In such circumstances, most of his colleagues would slap the siren on the roof and barrel through the traffic, all lights blazing. If he were being honest, Camille would have to admit that he too has given in to temptation. But only rarely. And not this time. He turns on the G.P.S. to look for an alternative route, fumbles with his glasses and drops them on the floor of the car; it takes an acrobatic feat to reach them and, naturally, it is at precisely this moment that his phone rings.

"Where are you?" Anne asks.

Camille releases the accelerator, the car shudders and stalls, he grabs for his glasses, wedges the phone against his shoulder and, now panting for breath, he gasps:

"Not far, not far . . ."

"Are you driving or sprinting?" Anne is amused.

Suddenly, the road ahead is clear. He clambers back

onto the driver's seat as horns honk impatiently behind him, tugs at his seat belt, keys the ignition, jerks the throttle, shifts into third gear, his mobile phone still wedged under his chin. The car judders.

"I'll be right there," he says, "five minutes . . ."

But he instantly drops the phone which clatters onto his knees and, of course, immediately rings again.

Traffic is moving smoothly now, a diversion has been opened up. Camille passes a frantic traffic cop whirling his baton and blowing his whistle like a madman. Camille is concentrating, careful not to lose his way. In fact, he is closer than he realised, just a few streets from Anne's apartment.

The screen on his phone flashes, indicating a call from Louis, his deputy. He cannot help but wonder what Louis is doing on the force. The guy is rich as Croesus, he could spend his whole life dozing by a swimming pool without ever having to worry about money. And he's an intellectual to boot, a walking encyclopaedia, no-one catches him out . . . But in spite of everything, he decided to work at the *Brigade criminelle*. Deep down, the guy's a romantic.

Camille takes the call.

Louis tells him about the explosion on the rue Joseph-Merlin.

"Yeah, I heard," Camille says.

He is looking for a parking spot, passes the building where Anne lives and is about to drive around the block again.

"The ministry is all over the place, the *Préfecture* is . . ."

"Come on, spit it out," says Camille.

He is nervous because he has just spotted an empty parking space ahead, and the prospect of parallel parking while juggling his mobile phone . . . He slows down, turns on the hazard lights.

"There's a man here," says Louis. "He's insisting on speaking to you."

"And that's why you're calling me? You deal with him."

"He says he'll only talk to you. He says he planted the bomb."

Camille stops. The car behind him flashes its headlights.

"Listen, Louis, there are always guys who . . ."

But Louis does not give him time to finish:

"He started filming the site of the blast a full minute before the explosion, so there's not much doubt. If he's not the bomber, he's bloody well-informed."

This time, Camille does not hesitate, he rolls down the window, sticks the siren on the roof, turns on the flashing lights and floors the accelerator.

"It's me," he says to Anne. "About tonight . . . I think we'll have to postpone."

7.45 p.m.

The police force was thrown into turmoil by the bombing, the *Brigade criminelle* was frantic; news of the arrival of the young man who claimed to have planted the bomb on the rue Joseph-Merlin has spread like wildfire.

On the ground floor, Camille runs into Basin, the guy

35

from the Crime Lab. They know each other, they have worked a couple of cases together, they get along well.

"The explosion was definitely caused by a 140-mm shell," Basin explains, walking Camille to the stairs.

"But . . . they're huge, those things."

Basin spreads his hands, as though indicating the size of the pike that got away.

"About 50 centimetres by . . . say, 14? No, not particularly big. Pretty heavy, though."

Camille mentally notes the information.

"And as far as damage is concerned, what do we know?"

"There are a number of factors." Basin reels off a list: "The presence of the scaffolding, the wooden walkway, the barrier created by the façade of the building, the depth at which the bomb was planted – that curbed the scope of the blast and the shockwave. But for these factors, the death toll could have been considerable. Imagine if he'd planted the shell under a cinema and set it to go off at nine o'clock, you'd be dealing with twenty fatalities."

He seems to reconsider, changes his mind.

"Make that thirty."

Basin turns and leaves, Camille heads on towards his office where he comes upon a young woman sitting in the corridor. Petrified. Two guards deployed, just for her.

"This is the only witness," says Louis, "Clémence Kriszewckanszki. I've arranged a lineup."

Camille goes into his office.

"O.K., Louis, tell me everything."

"His name is Garnier."

Holding his elegant notebook, his elegant pen, Louis pushes his fringe back with his right hand.

"Why the hell does he want to talk to me?" Camille says irritably. "Why not someone else?"

"He says he saw you on T.V."

"That gives us some idea of his intelligence . . ."

Louis does not rise to the bait and carries on:

"He's got no police record, but we've got one on his mother, Rose Garnier. She's been on remand for the past eight months, charged with murder."

"That gives us some idea of the family dynamic."

Camille takes the piece of paper Louis has proffered. A perfect, thirty-line précis. Camille can never remember which of the *grandes écoles* Louis was accepted to – E.N.A. or Normale Sup' – but it hardly matters since he didn't go to either, he joined the police force. Thirty lines outlining the case of mother Garnier. There is nothing on the son.

On his desk, photos of the attack taken a few minutes after the explosion. An apocalyptic scene. Images from the past resurface in Camille's mind, the terrorist attack on the rue des Rosiers, the one on the rue Copernic. What year were the Paris métro bombings? He never did have a good head for dates.

He lingers over the bewildered little boy sprawled on the pavement, his face covered in blood, one cheek pressed against the tarmac, in his hand a gaping, empty clarinet case.

It is the child victims Camille finds most upsetting, he feels a sort of kindred spirit with them, because of his height.

Then again, he has always been the sensitive type. The sort of cop who is easily moved to tears.

7.55 p.m.

Camille figures he must be about thirty.

"Twenty-seven. Last June," Jean corrects him, as though somehow it is important.

His eyes flit about the room, unable to settle. Hands between his knees, he slowly rubs his palms together, but this means nothing. Most people are embarrassed when they first see Camille, standing four feet eleven tall, having to stoop to look him in the eye, or see him sitting on a chair, his feet dangling inches off the floor. This young man knows Verhœven, to him, he is "as seen on T.V.", but face to face with the real Verhœven is a different matter.

And despite looking like a farm labourer, the boy is timid.

"Garnier, John," Camille announces.

"Jean!"

The young man starts forward, this detail seems important to him. Camille sceptically peers at the I.D. card, as though deciphering a foreign language:

"Sorry, to me it reads 'John'."

The young man glares at him.

"Alright, O.K.," says Camille, "it's spelled John but pronounced Jean. Well, now, *Jean*" – Camille stresses the word – "so you planted the bomb on the rue Joseph-Merlin."

He folds his arms.

"Tell me about that."

"There were roadworks. I planted the bomb before they refilled the hole."

Camille offers no reaction. In circumstances like these, suspects talk, they ramble on, contradict themselves, sometimes they fall apart. The best thing to do is let them talk.

"The mortar shell," Jean corrects himself. "I planted it at night."

Camille raises an eyebrow, sceptical. Jean (or John) has a deep voice that falters after the first few words, as though scattering full stops everywhere, resulting in rudimentary sentences, subject-verb-object.

"They were laying pipes. The road was up for a couple of days. There was a barrier. So no-one would fall into the hole. I went there one night, threw a tarpaulin over the trench, climbed down and worked under the tarp. I dug into the wall of the trench, planted the shell fifty centimetres below street level, rigged the detonator – it was an alarm clock – set it and then filled in the hole."

There's no mystery with this guy. On the contrary, he is happy to explain every detail, you only have to ask.

Louis is staring at his computer screen. A quick glance from Camille and he confirms: new pipes were laid on the rue Joseph-Merlin last month.

"And why did you do it?" Camille asks. "What do you want?"

But Jean does not respond to questions. He is prepared to tell all, but in his own time, things have to play out exactly as he imagined. He is meticulous.

39

"The mortar shells . . . I planted seven of them. There are six more. One explosion every day. That's how they're rigged."

"But . . ." Camille is dumbfounded. "What is it you want?"

Jean wants his mother (who is on remand) and himself (he is about to be taken into custody) to be released.

"Put us in, you know, in some sort of 'witness protection programme'."

It is foolish, but Camille's first reaction is to laugh. Jean is utterly impassive.

"You give us new identities," he continues. "You get us to Australia, give us money, enough to get us settled. I was thinking five million. As soon as we land, I'll tell you the location of the other six shells."

"That sort of thing happens in the United States," says Camille. "Not here! You've been watching too many American cop shows. This is France, and we . . ."

"Yeah, I know" – Jean makes a sweeping gesture, clearly irritated – *I know!* "But if they can do it over there, we can do it here. Actually, I'm pretty sure it's been done before. For spies and mafia informers and people like that, check it out. Not that it matters, that's the deal, take it or leave it . . ."

The young man may be naïve and he is obviously immature (running off to Australia is the sort of thing a kid might dream up), but he is far from stupid. And if the threat is genuine, the potential damage is incalculable.

"Alright," Camille says, getting to his feet. "Let's take that again from the top, if you don't mind."

No problem.

Jean is happy, the clearer things are, the sooner it will all be resolved.

"About the money, I could drop it to four million. But that's as low as I'll go."

He does not seem to have the slightest doubt.

8.05 p.m.

Stepping out of the interview room, Camille comes face to face with the girl with the unpronounceable name. He smiles and approaches her.

"Are you alright?"

She simply nods.

"We're going to need your help," Camille explains. "After that, you can go home."

She nods again. O.K.

Just before they go to do the lineup, Camille takes Louis aside.

"Go and pull Garnier out of there . . ."

Louis pushes back his fringe, a sign of embarrassment. This is not protoc—

"Yeah, I know, Louis," Camille cuts him off. "But I don't give a shit. If he's our guy, whether we've followed protocol will be the least of our worries. Shift it."

And so, as young Clémence looks through the one-way mirror at the five men with no belts, no laces, no ties, young men, old men, five officers from various branches of the force, she shakes her head, she is sorry, but honestly . . .

"It's not one of them," she says confidently.

Her voice is charming, soft-spoken, she forces a smile, she would have liked to help, she wishes she had been able to recognise the young man . . . She is asked to look at them again but, no, the man she saw on the café terrace is not there.

Camille shrugs as if to say, oh well, can't win them all.

Then he opens the door and, naturally, as soon as she steps out into the corridor, Clémence turns to the *commandant* as though about to run the other way. She jerks her thumb behind her, signalling the boy sitting on the bench between two plain-clothes officers, the three of them looking like patients in a doctor's waiting room.

"That's him!" she hisses between clenched teeth. "That's him!"

This is both good news, and the beginning of his problems. Camille asks one of the plain-clothes officers to take Clémence home.

Before he goes back to his office, he calls the switchboard and asks to be put through to Basin. Around him, everyone falls silent, the presence of the man who claims to have carried out the attack has everyone electrified, they are waiting for confirmation.

"So?" Basin's voice on the other end of the line.

"I don't want to say too much," Camille whispers, "but I think this could be really serious. I need you to come and hear him out . . . to tell me . . . from a technical viewpoint." Camille walks towards the window, trying to collect his thoughts. "He says there are six more bombs. One explosion every day."

However much he says the word, "explosion" is like "tsunami" or "earthquake" – you know it implies carnage but unless you are actually there, it remains an abstract concept.

8.15 p.m.

Jean Garnier watches Camille come back into the office. He is accompanied by a tall, broad-shouldered man with oddly feminine hands who takes a chair, sits behind him and folds his arms. It does not seem to bother Jean.

They start again from the beginning.

"So you're saying you bought seven mortar shells?"

"No," Jean says. "I didn't buy them. I collected them along the Souain-Perthes road, near Sommepy. And in Monthois."

Camille looks over Jean's shoulder and Basin gives a curt nod. It is an area in eastern France, he will later explain, near Châlons, in the département de Marne. Dozens of shells from the First World War turn up there every year; farmers leave them by the roadside for bomb disposal experts to collect.

Camille is poleaxed.

This man simply picked up mortar shells by the road-side.

"And how did you transport them?"

Jean turns towards Louis' desk where they laid out the contents of the sports bag he was carrying when he arrived. He stretches his arm out, points to a sheaf of receipts held together by a paperclip.

"I rented a car. The receipt is in there."

When Basin speaks, Jean does not turn, he remains focussed. Basin wants to know the technical details. It is one thing to find a mortar shell, a very different thing to set it off.

"A detonator and an electrical relay," Jean says as though it were obvious. "It's not rocket science."

He points to a digital calendar-clock.

"I rigged all the bombs with one of those. €3.99 on the internet."

Louis takes a receipt from the sheaf; Garnier paid by debit card, the card is in his wallet, there can be no doubt. This is the first time they have ever seen a criminal bring receipts to prove his guilt.

Jean gestures to a box filled with detonators, slim tubes about the length of a cigarette.

"I stole those from Technic'Alpes," he explains. "They provide materials to public works contractors in Haute-Savoie."

Louis keys the name into a search engine.

"They only have one part-time security guard," Jean says. "It wasn't particularly difficult."

"The company exists," Louis confirms, looking at his monitor, "their headquarters are in Cluses."

"The headquarters might be," says Jean, "but the warehouse is in Sallanches."

Everyone in the room is beginning to feel extremely uneasy.

If he is telling the truth about the bomb on the rue Joseph-Merlin, he is probably telling the truth about the others. The six mortar shells still out there. Basin obviously believes this and is nodding constantly at Camille. As far as he is concerned, there is no doubt. Technically, the guy is completely capable.

Basin gets up, walks around Jean Garnier's chair and stands, staring down at him.

"The reason people turn up mortar shells from the First World War is because they haven't exploded. Only about one in four is actually operational."

Jean's brow furrows. He does not understand.

"I mean," Basin explains patiently, "that your threat is only a threat if the shells are functional. Do you understand?"

Basin talks as though speaking to a simpleton or a deaf-mute. It is hard to fault him for this; Jean Garnier does not have a face that radiates intelligence.

Basin continues, pedantically:

"You cannot be sure that your shells will explode. Therefore, your threat—"

"First off," Jean interrupts, counting on his fingers, "the first one worked pretty well. And secondly: that's why I planted six more, to allow for the ones that won't explode. And thirdly: if you're happy to take that risk, that's fine by me."

Silence.

Basin tries to regain his composure.

"Everything you used is here?"

"The electrical relays, the wiring, I bought all that at Leroy-Merlin," says Jean.

No-one reacts, but Jean does not care, he has decided to tell all.

"Oh, yeah ... You won't find a computer at my place, I dumped it. I know that you can recover data even if the hard drive has been erased, so ... "

The same goes for his mobile phone, he cancelled the contract months ago.

Camille is having trouble taking everything in. He needs to review the situation with Basin and Louis.

He leaves Jean in the custody of an officer, he could just as easily leave him on his own; they all agree there is no danger.

They step out into the corridor.

"Fucking hell . . ." says Camille as the door swings closed. "You're telling me it's possible to terrorise a whole city with alarm clocks bought online, some wiring from Leroy-Merlin, and a bunch of mortar shells picked up on the side of the road?"

Basin shrugs.

"Yeah. Easy. During the Great War, more than a billion shells were fired and one in four of them was buried in the ground without exploding. They're still rising to the surface like dead fish, you only have to bend down and pick them up. We've recovered twenty-five million, in other words, fuck all. If we carry on at this rate, it would take seven hundred years to recover the rest of them ... Most are inoperative, but then again, there are a hell of a lot of them. If you have seven, then, statistically, there's a good chance you have at least one or two that are still functional. If you're lucky, you might have three, four, even five. Obviously, if they're all functional, you've hit the jackpot.

"He used a digital alarm clock as a trigger, but anything capable of producing an electrical pulse could be used as a detonator: a doorbell, a mobile phone . . ."

This is all news to Camille.

"People assume that terrorism is sophisticated," says Basin. "Actually, it's not."

8.45 p.m.
Bustle is followed by commotion. While information filters through the tortuous channels of state hierarchy, the *Brigade criminelle* does not hang around, they get to work.

Divisionnaire Le Guen, a pachyderm of Shakespearean proportions simply in terms of weight, but one with a razor-sharp intelligence, contacts the *juge d'instruction* appointed to oversee the case. They are agreed on one thing: Commandant Camille Verhœven will lead the investigation "until the requisite special measures can be put in place".

Camille looks at his watch and laughs.

"Which will take, what? an hour?"

Louis reckons at least two, but they agree it will be swift. Camille's brief is simply to do the spadework. After that, he will be sidelined; but he does not envy his successor, this case stinks to high heaven.

For the time being, however, fifteen other officers have been seconded to his team. Louis has been busy putting them in the picture. By the time Camille arrives, they know why they are there. As soon as he comes into the room, the chattering stops. He usually has this effect, his theatrical smallness, his gleaming bald pate, but especially his eyes, a look that is sharp as a blade. And he can be theatrical: in the gravest circumstances, he is a man of few words. And so everyone falls silent; he marks a pause for a few seconds. A little melodramatic, perhaps, but no-one objects. Everyone here knows him, they know about his past, his wife, the depression, his enforced sabbatical and his return . . . Verhœven is little short of legendary.

He succinctly describes the self-professed culprit while Louis hands out the case summary he has typed up, precise, well argued, impeccable.

"If Garnier is telling the truth," says Camille, "a second bomb should explode in the next twenty-four hours. And since the incident on the rue Joseph-Merlin was no joke, we need to take the threat very seriously."

He might have added something momentous like "The first bomb resulted in no fatalities, that in itself is a miracle. It is our job to deal with the second . . .", but contrary to what Garnier believes, reality has very little in common with cop shows.

Camille simply offers a warning:

"I don't know yet how the authorities will decide to manage the affair, but in the meantime, there must be no communication with the media or with anyone else

48

for that matter. I shouldn't have to remind you, this is a tight-knit team . . ."

He allows a silence to ripple through the room, one that everyone present clearly understands: anyone who leaks information will be in deep shit.

But Camille is under no illusions. The media are baying for blood, the fact that Jean Garnier surrendered himself will leak before long; expecting a secret of this magnitude to be kept is sheer fantasy.

"I want you to comb through Jean Garnier's past, his friends, his relatives, etc. And especially what he was doing yesterday, the day before yesterday and the day before that, who he saw, who he bumped into, any contact he had within the neighbourhood. We're aiming to retrace his movements over the past few weeks."

Camille decides on the teams, apportions responsibilities, and concludes:

"Louis Mariani will be coordinating the investigation, anything that turns up – anything – goes through him. Right, good luck."

Then he makes his way through the canteen to meet with the *juge*.

Louis immediately gathers the various teams together, the officers jostle and heckle. In his elegant Armani suit, he may look like a princeling, but he is astonishingly efficient. He responds to their queries calmly and precisely, he looks as though he could parry questions all night without breaking a sweat.

Twenty minutes later, everyone has disappeared and

Louis has retired to the Comms room, ready to take calls from the officers out in the field, sift through the information, pin images and information to the corkboard, write progress reports for the *divisionnaire*, the *juge* and Camille.

9.10 p.m.

Camille spent the whole journey clutching his seat belt. It was impossible to think, what with the flashing lights and sirens. The driver is a boy racer who didn't see the need to hit the brakes more than once or twice between Paris and Bagnolet.

But Camille was insistent in his orders and so, a few minutes from Jean's house, the lights and sirens are switched off, the convoy slows and allows Verhœven's car to move in front; the forensics team will work discreetly, no need to panic the whole neighbourhood, they need to move quickly but quietly.

The housing estate where Rosie and Jean Garnier live is a drab collection of buildings. Considered poor in the 1970s, it was deemed middle class a decade later and these days, tenanted by thirtysomethings, millenials and middle managers, it aspires to the status of a "gated community". And in fact, that is what people are supposed to call it. Not housing estate, but *gated community*. There are no plebs here.

Number 21 is the first building on the left. There are cars everywhere. The estate was not built for thirtysome-thing environmentalists who love their hybrids, and so the police cars are forced to double-park. Camille waves them on, go and wait down there. But though they try to be discreet, as soon as they arrive at the door, they hear footsteps echoing in the concrete stairwell, as neighbours appear, four of them, then five, perched on the stairs like chickens, waiting for someone to summon the nerve to go and find out what is going on. They whisper amongst themselves, everyone has heard something, everyone has an opinion. Camille asks a colleague to go and interview them, to ask them what they think about their neighbours, obviously they are overjoyed . . .

Camille steps inside, and two officers and two forensics technicians run into the apartment.

The blinds are drawn, various plants have been placed in the bathtub which is half filled; upended plastic bottles have been pushed into the pots of those plants that are easily overwatered. The place is spick and span, the unplugged fridge is empty, the door left open, the beds are made, the wardrobes neat, the floors have been meticulously vacuumed. The air is thick with the smell of all-purpose household detergent, furniture polish and the whole arsenal of retail industrial cleaning products.

The furniture is old, but in very good condition: in the living room, there is a teak table with matching chairs that might have been fashionable thirty years ago, a sideboard in which the best china is carefully arranged. On the glass shelves of a display cabinet, there are rows of ornaments, horses made from spun glass, holiday souvenirs, a doll in traditional dress whose country of origin Camille cannot work out. In the modest bookcase, there are cheap book club editions, faux-leather with gilt-embossed titles (Zola's *Rougon-Macquart* series, *Great Battles of France*, *Secrets of the Knights Templar* . . .) not one of which has ever been opened. While the forensics officers go through the cupboards, Camille takes a look at Rosie's room. The bed is crowded with soft toys of the kind you might win at a funfair, all seemingly awaiting her return. On the floor, a bedside rug in fake fur. An astonishing number of Harlequin romances are carefully lined up on a shelf (*Guilty Passion*, *The Bridge to Happiness*, *One Night of Magic* . . .) As he leaves the room, Camille pauses to study a suitcase one of the officers has just taken from the wardrobe. The contents smell of memories. Camille casts a quick eye over it.

"Bag all this up for me," he says.

Jean's room: football posters on the walls, a vast library of video games and horror movies. Here, too, everything is perfectly arranged, there is not a thing out of place.

The apartment belongs to the local Affordable Housing Association. With Jean Garnier under arrest, within two months it will be cleared out and offered to a new family, everything here will end up in a skip. Whether the tenants were planning to come back or whether they had left for good seems immaterial; either way, the apartment was perfectly prepared for a police raid.

The prospect that Jean Garnier has planted six more bombs primed to go off seems suddenly more credible.

9.45 p.m.

Initial witness statements give the impression of a young man who was timid but always ready to lend a hand.

"He used to come round and do D.I.Y.," according to a neighbour (she is fat, fifty, potbellied and priggish). "Replace a tap, rewire a plug, that kind of thing, anything to make a little money . . . He wasn't exactly the talkative type, yes ma'am, no ma'am, that was about the extent of his conversation. You wouldn't invite him round for a chat. But a nice lad. Wouldn't harm a fly."

"As far as flies go, I'm with you," says Camille. "Not a single fly died on the rue Joseph-Merlin."

The young man handcuffed to the steel table is exhausted. He was officially charged two hours ago, and in those two hours, he has endured a barrage of questions from a series of officers working in ten- to fifteen-minute shifts.

While Camille was meeting with his superiors, the colleagues who took over roughed Jean up a little. He is clutching his stomach, there is a large bruise on his left cheek, a deep gash on his forehead, he is having trouble breathing. "He had a fall in the corridor," they told Camille.

When it comes to terrorist offences, the police have a wide range of legal weapons at their disposal, there is no maximum period of custody, it can drag on for half a century. The officers take advantage of the rules: Jean will not be seeing his lawyer any time soon. Not that it matters, Jean says he doesn't want one.

"Mind telling us why?" Camille asks.

"Don't need one. You give me what I want, I'll give you what you want, job done. Otherwise, hundreds of people will die and I'll get life without parole. I don't see how a lawyer could help . . ."

He strokes his cheek.

"Your colleagues got a bit heavy-handed, but you need me if you're going to find the other bombs, so . . ."

The gesture stops Camille in his tracks.

Because Jean is fine. He's more than fine, given the circumstances.

Over the course of his career, Camille has seen his fair share of police brutality, he has seen a suspect's every possible reaction, and what alarms him in this case is that Jean has been badly beaten but behaves as though it were the most normal thing in the world, as though he has been expecting it, anticipating the reaction of the police.

How much has he anticipated?

He seems astonishingly broody and sullen for a man capable of devising such an elaborate plan.

Is there something not quite right here?

"John Garnier," Camille reads aloud. "Semi-professional footballer, diploma in electromechanical engineering. Known to be a good handyman. Odd jobs . . . Short periods of unemployment."

Jean has a face that marks easily. The bruise is already beginning to turn purple. Camille scans the file in front of him, then looks up, admiringly.

"So you still live with your mother. At the age of twenty-seven."

Jean does not respond to this remark

"'Father unknown' . . . come on, Jean, tell me a little about that."

"'Father unknown' means I never knew my father, what do you want me to say?"

"Yes, but that's just something they put on your birth certificate. What I'm interested in is what Rosie told you."

"He didn't want anything to do with me, that's his right."

Without realising, Garnier has raised his voice. He must have said this same sentence hundreds of times in the past twenty-seven years, that sort of pat answer designed to avoid the truth, to make it easier not to think about it, to overcome the problem.

"You're spot-on," Camille says. "That is his right."

Anyone who did not know Verhœven would think he was being sincere. Silence.

"He couldn't marry my mother," Jean says, his voice calmer now. "He wanted to but he couldn't, so he went abroad. That's all."

"Madame Garnier and her son? They argued a lot . . ."

This from the upstairs neighbour, she lives alone and has numerous cats. A suspicious woman. Unlike the others, who were only too happy to get their pictures in the paper, she refused to open her door until she had telephoned the *commissariat* to verify the officer's identity.

Even then, she would not allow the female officer across the threshold.

"Do you have any idea what they argued about?"

"Everything, nothing. Every day they were at it! Well, almost every day . . . I must have gone down and banged on their door a dozen times, but they never answered. The next day, she'd set off to work like nothing had happened. As for him, he never so much as said 'good morning'. Smashing crockery and slamming doors and calling each other every name under the sun until all hours!"

She shakes her head as though she were shocked just listening to herself. Then she closes the door.

"At least since she's been in prison we've had a bit of peace in the building."

"You and your mother couldn't stand each other," Camille says, "so it's strange that you would be happy to plant seven bombs to get her released. Since you've been here, you haven't even asked to see her . . . I'm sorry, Jean, but your story just doesn't make sense."

"You don't have to make sense of it," Jean says without looking up. "You just let us go and I'll tell you where the shells are planted."

Camille catches him glancing at the wall clock.

"So the next bomb, what time is it set to go off tomorrow?"

Jean breaks into a thin-lipped smile.

"You're making a mistake taking me for a fool. You'll change your tune, just wait and see."

He is offered nothing to eat, he asks for nothing; he has not touched the bottle of water and the glass in front of him. He stares at the floor, he already has the ashen pallor of a suspect approaching the end of his tether, but he is holding up.

Camille leafs through the case file of his mother, Rosie Garnier.

Two years ago, Jean fell in love with Carole Wendlinger, a 23-year-old from Alsace. She dreams of going back there. He dreams of Carole. They decide to go together.

"I totally get it," Camille says suddenly.

Carole looks pretty in the photograph, with her ash-blonde hair, her broad smile, her blue eyes.

Marie-Christine Hamrouche, forty years old, Rosie's colleague and her best friend. She gave a statement on the day Rosie was arrested and probably testified at her trial, but she enjoys telling this story, she never tires of it.

"You have to understand, Rosie was always complaining about her son . . . Not a day went by that they didn't have a quarrel, a shouting match, it was never-ending. He would never do the shopping, but if she didn't bring back exactly what he wanted, he'd blow his top. They were always at each other's throats, about what was on television, about his dirty laundry, the plants that needed watering, the jobs that needed doing around the house, the overflowing ashtrays . . . Every day it was something different. I used to say to her, to listen to you, you'd be better off with a husband, at least he'd bring home his pay packet."

The officer nods sagely, thinking about his own wife.

"And as for Jean, if you wanted to get him to do a hand's turn you had to get up early. So when he met that girl of his, we all hoped it would work out for them. I swear, when he said he was moving away with her, Rosie was delighted. You'd think she was the one who'd had a wedding proposal. It was a relief . . . As much for us as for her, I have to say, her colleagues I mean, because Rosie and her son were so wound up that sooner or later things were bound to end badly . . ."

She trails off. At this point in the story, words always fail her, she looks at the officer, her eyes wide.

"So when we heard the news, well, I tell you we were shocked."

"So let me get this straight, Jean," Camille says. "And correct me if I'm wrong. You and your mother fight like cat and dog, but even though she bitches about you all the time, the thought of losing you, of being on her own, is too much for her to bear. No-one knows exactly how it happens, but I'm guessing that she resists, she cries, she stamps her feet, but since this gets her nowhere, since you're determined to stick with Carole, she pretends to give up, she's secretly seething and one night, as your girl-friend is coming home after her shift at the supermarket, your mother runs her over with the car. Killed outright. Your little Carole dreamed of the Alsace of her childhood, and now she's pushing up daisies in the cemetery in Pantin. Your mother hides the car. A month later, there's a bizarre combination of circumstances, a fire breaks out in the basement in the middle of the day, and since the owners are not around, firefighters break open a number of the locked garages and find the car. End of story. Is that about right, Jean?"

It's hard to tell whether or not Jean is listening, he looks more like a man waiting for a train.

"When your mother is arrested, you're hauled in for questioning . . . Hardly surprising – the car used to murder your girlfriend has been found in the family lock-up, that makes you look like the perfect accomplice, but the *juge* doesn't hold it against you; you never use the car, they never find your fingerprints inside, and anyway you and Carole were planning to take off together, so they're hardly likely to think you were involved in her murder . . ."

Jean does not flicker an eyelash.

"Except that now, everything has changed. Because you're trying to get your mother set free. Obviously, you're not one to hold a grudge, so you've got that in your favour. But in hindsight, it sheds new light on Carole's death. And it's likely to put you back in the frame, because the idea that you were somehow complicit, well, the *juge* is going to love that."

Jean stares at the wall and sighs, irritated that he is forced to repeat himself.

"If I set off six more bombs in the middle of the city, it's hardly going to make much difference."

"But your mother killed your girlfriend, Jean! Why are you so determined to defend her?"

"Because it's not fair!" Jean screams. "She acted on impulse!"

He falls silent, as though he is sorry that he got carried away, that he revealed something so private.

"What I mean is . . . it's not her fault."

The pressure subsides, but in those few seconds Camille got a glimpse of something crucial, something that may well explain Jean Garnier's behaviour: his anger. A rage that, like his mother's rage on the day she went out and ran Carole down, flared into fury. Except that in Jean's case, he choked back his rage. And it gave birth to a grisly plan, a cold, calculating plan to sow terror. Garnier is out of his depth.

"All the more reason . . . if it's not her fault."

Garnier frowns. Camille patiently explains.

"If you think that there are mitigating circumstances, why wouldn't you let her go to trial? You testify in her defence, the psychiatrists explain that it was a moment of madness, that she is not legally responsible . . ."

"And they throw her in a mental asylum, thanks but no thanks."

Camille moves his chair closer.

"Listen, Jean. Your first bomb caused only minor injuries, but you're not always going to be so lucky." (He feels like adding "and neither are we", but he does not.) "Right now, the authorities are assessing the situation. You wanted to talk to me, and for the time being, they're

O.K. with that, but unless I get results pretty quickly, and by that I mean right now, they're going to kick things up a gear . . . And I can tell you right now, the guys they're going to hand you over to are no jokers."

He comes closer still, Jean leans his head forward, as though to hear a secret.

"I'm telling you, Jean, these guys are vicious bastards . . ."

He moves back. Garnier is pale. His lower lip is trembling slightly.

"There's no point in persisting, Jean. No-one is ever going to give in to your demands."

Garnier swallows hard.

"We'll see," he says simply, "you'll see . . ."

10.05 p.m.
The *juge* was prompt. Rosie Garnier, forty-six, postal delivery worker, incarcerated in Fleury-Mérogis, was extricated double-quick.

They sat her on a chair in an empty office. There is not another stick of furniture in the room, anyone wanting to sit opposite her would have to bring another chair. And this is what Camille did. They are metal chairs, heavy as a dead donkey; he did not so much carry it as drag it behind him, the shriek of metal on concrete made Rosie's eyes narrow. Then he climbed onto it, like a character in a David Lynch film.

Camille opens the file in his lap. He looks at the photograph of Rosie taken a year earlier, just after she was sentenced. Today, she is twenty kilos lighter, but looks at least ten years older, her face is gaunt, haggard, she has bags under her eyes like bruises, she is clearly not sleeping or eating much. Only a man could fantasise about women's prisons. Her badly cut hair is white and grey, she looks as though she is wearing a dusty wig.

Rosie.

The case file explains it. It was her father who gave her the name in 1964, the year when his idol, Gilbert Bécaud, released the single "Rosy and John". Moved by this gesture, Rosie carried on the tradition and named her son John.

"He never liked it . . ." she told the *juge*. "But it's a lovely song."

Camille does not mince words.

"Your son claims he's planted seven bombs," he says. "The first obliterated half a street in the eighteenth arrondissement and there are six more. He's promising there will be a bloodbath."

Camille is not sure that she understands what he is saying. He settles on the most expedient method: close off every possible avenue.

"He says he'll tell us where the bombs are if we agree to release you, you and him. And it is impossible to set you free. Absolutely impossible."

Rosie has some difficulty digesting this information: the bombs, her son, being released, impossible. Camille drives home the last nail.

"The only thing Jean will get is life without parole."

He leans back in his chair as though he is finished, as though the rest is none of his business.

Rosie shakes her head. She is talking to herself.

"He's not a bad lad, my Jean . . ."

She cannot imagine her son doing such a thing. Still, Camille does not move. It takes almost a minute before the penny drops, the blood drains from her face, and her lips part with a pained, almost inaudible "oh". Time for Camille to take the reins again.

"If you help us, the judge will take that into account at his trial, and at yours. But it's him I'm thinking about mostly. Knocking a girl off a moped, even deliberately, is one thing; planting bombs around Paris is a very different matter. You could well be released in a couple of years, but if another one of those bombs goes off, Jean will never get out. Never. He is twenty-seven, and he's facing fifty years in prison."

Rosie is listening carefully, she understands.

Camille read her psychiatrist's assessment. Not exactly Einstein. Very little education, limited ability, poor judgement, inclined to make impulsive decisions, chaotic affective responses, emotions entirely channelled into her relationship with her son . . . He studies her and finds his initial reaction confirmed. She is a stupid woman. It is always a difficult judgement to pass, you feel a niggling compassion, almost a sense of shame.

Camille has a momentary doubt.

"These bombs. Did you know about them?"

"He never tells me anything, my Jean!"

She formulates it as a general complaint, as though talking about some domestic problem.

63

"Madame Garnier, do you fully understand what is going on here?"

"Can I talk to him?"

This is the big question. The *juge* thinks they should meet as soon as possible. Camille is not so sure.

"Can I see Jean?" she persists. "Talk to him . . ."

Technically, the *juge* is right, it is obvious that the two of them should be allowed to talk. His mother is the only leverage they have with Jean, probably the only person in the world who can convince him.

And yet Camille cannot decide. There is something odd in Rosie's voice. Something not quite right, and until he has managed to work out what it is . . .

"We'll see," he says. "We'll see."

He tells the *juge* he believes a meeting might be counterproductive.

"The mother is in a bad way, she's been badly damaged by her time in prison. This must be one of the things he's worried about because he went to visit her when she was first on remand, but he never went back . . . He writes to her every week, but that's their only contact. If he sees her in this state, there's a serious risk it will simply reinforce his demand to get her out of there . . ."

The magistrate agrees. They will wait and see.

10.15 p.m.

"Six more shells? One explosion a day? That's what you're telling me?"

The information is having trouble percolating.

"And he wants his mother?"

"That's correct, *Monsieur le premier ministre*. His mother."

"He thinks we'll pack him off to Australia and wait for a postcard with the location of the bombs. Is he thick or what?"

So it is decided: a media blackout. No-one knows whether this is a good decision, but at the moment it seems the only choice there is between various bad decisions.

"Come up with an official explanation for the explosion," says the prime minister. "Something everyone can understand. Put together a draft communiqué, I don't care how you go about it. We have to play for time, and in the meantime you –" he turns to the counterterrorism officer – ". . . do whatever you have to do."

As he is about to leave the room, he turns back.

"Just put an end to this bullshit!"

Once he is gone, the principal private secretary offers a free translation.

"Put Jean Garnier's balls in a vice. And turn the screws."

The counterterrorism agent gets up and leaves without a word.

Silence. Everyone can tell all hell is about to break loose.

Yet no-one can say why. Perhaps it is the suddenness and the severity of the situation, perhaps the speed at which events are unfolding means one tends to envisage disastrous outcomes which, in politics, are usually the most likely to ensue.

The authorities have a whole panoply of crisis response plans and disaster recovery strategies detailing how emergency services should respond in the event of major incidents. While they wait to see whether or not Garnier will come clean, they need to act. It may be necessary to trigger the O.R.S.E.C. civil emergencies plan; they need to begin a detailed survey and analysis of the potential risks posed by the series of explosions and establish operational and mobilisation conditions . . .

10.40 p.m.

Witness statements continue to come in, but Louis has not been able to reconstruct the movements of Jean Garnier over the past weeks.

"He barely sees anyone," Louis tells Camille. "His only friends are the guys he plays football with, and none of them have seen him for weeks. According to the neighbours, ever since his mother's arrest, he has been in and out of the apartment, they have bumped into him shopping for groceries, but no-one has noticed anything unusual. I sent teams to interview staff at every place he made a purchase, at the agency where he hired the car . . . But Jean is the sort of customer nobody notices and no-one remembers."

Ever since Clémence formally identified Jean Garnier, everyone on the team is agreed: they need to circulate his photograph, call for witnesses. But there is a media blackout. Orders from the ministry. The authorities are categorical. A photograph of the bomber in the morning newspapers would create panic.

"On the one hand you've got panic, and the other you've got carnage," Camille says. "I wouldn't like to be in the shoes of whoever's making the decisions."

"Pretty soon the relief team will get here and he'll be undergoing enhanced interrogation techniques, not many people can withstand that kind of grilling."

"It won't make any difference, he'll hold out to the bitter end," Camille says to Louis as they go to the coffee machine. "His plan is simple, it's black and white. His logic is implacable because it's simplistic, it's impervious to nuance. As far as he's concerned it's yes or no. The specialist interrogators will get nowhere, I'd put money on it."

As they wait for the relief team, Camille checks his watch more and more frequently, eager to be out of this mess.

Four men burst through the doors without even knocking.

The counterterrorism brigade is taking over.

They are all built like brick outhouses. Everything about them inspires fear: their manner, their determination, the preciseness of their movements. Jean Garnier stares at them, petrified. He has anticipated much of what would happen, and thus far everything has gone according to plan, but now the script has changed. Within seconds, he is hauled to his feet, arms twisted behind his back, handcuffed, hooded, shackled, restrained. Surrounded by the four men, he seems to have shrunk ten centimetres.

The message is clear: this is a serious gear change.

Camille does not smile, but he is relieved. Less than thirty seconds after they burst into his office, the specialists disappear with Garnier in tow.

Camille calls to the senior officer, Commandant Pelletier, a tall, square-jawed man with a salt-and-pepper moustache that dates from a previous century.

"Have fun . . ."

Pelletier remains focussed. He is clearly in his element. He is the last to leave. He has not uttered a single word.

11.15 p.m.

Camille gets in his car and sets off for Anne's apartment, but half-way there, feeling uneasy, he stops and takes out his mobile phone.

This thing is dragging on – he texts her – *Sorry . . . Maybe later tonight . . . O.K.?*

He does not think before he sends it. It is not that he does not want to be with her, on the contrary, he would like to lie next to her, caress her body, smell her perfume . . . but he is puzzled, preoccupied. There is something amiss, something he cannot put his finger on. His thoughts flicker back to the counterterrorist unit; in a case such as this he does not like to think what they might be capable of. They will know what to do.

And yet . . .

Doesn't matter how late – Anne texts back – *just come.*

Camille hesitates a moment; no, he will keep up his lie to Anne. He will go home.

Predictably, Doudouche is sulking. Camille is attentive, but to no avail, it is always like this when he comes home late, she pretends he does not exist.

Exhausted, he slumps fully clothed on the sofa but cannot get to sleep; letting Anne down, lying to her, upsets him. Especially since he didn't need to. Or maybe he did. It would have meant he was unavailable "You're off the case now," he tells himself, not that it makes any difference. He sits on the sofa, Doudouche on his lap, drawing (he never stops, there are roughs and sketches everywhere, it helps him to think, it is something he has always done, he replicates what he has seen from memory, which means he only really understands them in hindsight).

In his job, there are the facts, and the effect the facts have on him. It is not that he blindly trusts his own gut feeling, in fact he is more the type to be overcome by doubt, yet he listens to his hunches, his instincts, he cannot do otherwise.

And so here he is, doodling, trying to capture Rosie's face and, next to it, the face of John. The first portrait exudes a sort of simple-minded stubbornness, the second is more complex. There is stubbornness here too, but it is more calculating. Determination is a trait they have in common. In her, it appears as intransigence; in him, as single-mindedness. They may not look like much, but they are as dangerous as the black plague.

Looking at the portraits, Camille speculates about the relationship between them.

Rosie kills her son's girlfriend, he plans a wave of bombings to free her . . . Put side by side, these two isolated portraits do not compute. There is a glaring disparity. "You're off the case now." Good for you.

Not so for Jean Garnier, right now he will be going through hell. Camille has to stop drawing, because even what little he knows of enhanced interrogation techniques makes him shudder. No-one ever talks about them, but it doesn't take a genius to know that when someone threatens to set off bombs all over Paris, they're bound to pull out all the stops. He thinks: waterboarding, walling, stress positions, cramped confinement, heavy metal played on continuous loop . . . Do these things really exist?

Think about something else, try a different viewpoint. This is one of Camille's techniques. Any investigation throws a certain light on things, so Camille attempts to come at it from the opposite perspective. From memory, he re-creates a photograph glimpsed in Rosie Garnier's police file; a picture of Carole taken after she was mowed down. He sketches her hair, an almost perfect halo that seems unbearably cruel against the pool of blood shining in the harsh forensic glare. It looks like the hair of a little girl. For some reason, a dead girl with blonde hair is more upsetting. He traces the heartrending curve of her neck.

Then, finally, he drifts into unconsciousness with Doudouche curled up on his belly.

When the telephone rings just before four in the morning, he realises why he did not go round to Anne's apartment, why he did not go to bed.

His intuition did not fail him.

Doudouche refuses to budge, Camille pushes her off but she mewls in protest. His very bones ache with tiredness, but he struggles to his feet and lifts the receiver with one hand while the other fumbles with the buttons of his shirt: he needs to take a shower, and quickly.

It is the *juge*. Camille was expecting the call. He has to go back to work. Jean Garnier is refusing to talk to the counterterrorism agents, which comes as no surprise. He wants to talk to Verhœven, no-one else. Camille has only one question: why are they giving in to his demands?

"Because it's urgent," says the investigating magistrate. "Garnier is claiming that the next bomb is scheduled to go off at 3 p.m., we've got less than twelve hours."

As soon as he hangs up, Camille calls and wakes Louis, the indispensible Louis, who also has to get up and come back to the station.

"I don't get it," says Louis. "It's not exactly news that a bomb will go off in the next twelve hours. Garnier said there would be one bomb a day."

"I know," Camille says. "I don't know exactly what our friends from counterterrorism did, and frankly I don't want to know, but Garnier started to make a confession, then suddenly he clammed up, he won't talk to anyone but me, he says it's non-negotiable."

"So did he say where it is, the second bomb?"

"Yeah, that's why they've called us in. Garnier says he planted it in a school."

DAY TWO

DAY TWO

4.55 a.m.

Sitting with his arms folded, chin jutting, Pelletier, the head of the counterterrorism squad, treats being taken off the case as a snub. As Camille comes into the room and he gets to his feet, he all but stands on tiptoe to look down on him from an even greater height. Verhœven has been dealing with such slights for fifty years and though he still finds them irritating, it would take more than this to wind him up, and he is too tired to fight. Besides, he thinks the rivalry between law enforcement agencies is a bit of a cliché. Even so, he stares down Pelletier. From below, unavoidably. Counterterrorism is not a department, it's a vocation; we are not cops, we're highly trained specialists; if C.T. can't get a result, then no-one can. These are just some of the messages Pelletier is conveying with this stare.

Camille is genuinely sympathetic. After all, he himself has been taken off cases, or threatened with being taken off too many times.

But he does not have time to hang around, he still has to deal with the other. Given his importance, we will capitalise him: the Other. If Pelletier is openly hostile, the Other exudes quiet self-assurance and the muted reserve

75

of ministerial chambers; it is 5.00 a.m. but the Other is bright as a button, depressingly young, a senior post and not yet thirty, a potent brew of family connections, raw talent, willpower, hard graft, ambition and luck, the sort of cocktail that sticks in your craw. The hair, the suit, the shoes, the watch, the demeanour, even the way he clears his throat, everything is part of his personal image. Camille closes his eyes and shakes the desiccated hand. At least Commandant Pelletier's anger and frustration makes him seem like a normal human being . . .

It is at this point in Camille's assessment that Louis steps into the office.

The world abruptly shifts on its axis, the whole world; Jean Garnier's bomb must have produced a similar effect. Pelletier does not turn a hair, but in a nanosecond the Other grows pale, he shrinks, he shrivels, if he carries on like this he will be no taller than Camille. He stammers a few words as he approaches Louis, the two men share a brusque man-hug. Louis smiles serenely, turns to Camille and jerks his thumb at the Other.

"We sat the entrance exam for the E.N.A. together," he explains.

A little later, Camille will learn that Louis was first in his year, while the Other was at the back of the pack; it is the kind of inferiority complex even success cannot expunge. Louis gives the man a brusque nod. Go ahead, we're all ears.

Alright, the counterterrorism squad has done its best, blah, blah, blah (he does not even glance at Pelletier; no time for losers), but we have to be "realistic", the minister in person blah, blah, blah, strategic policy, critical juncture for the government, blah, blah, blah . . . Camille quickly loses interest, he does not even wait for the end.

"Yeah, O.K." he mutters, and, without warning, turns on his heel, leaves the room, strides down the hall, opens a door . . . Initially taken aback, the others quickly follow only to crash into him; the four men stand in the doorway, frozen: Jean Garnier is not a pretty sight.

He has obviously gone fifteen rounds with trained interrogators.

Camille gropes for a word: stunned? senseless? punch-drunk? stupefied? All of the above, but also beaten to a bloody pulp; the bruises are a vivid purple, only his swollen face is visible, the injuries hidden by his clothes can be guessed.

Camille studies Jean and there is something definitely amiss.

What?

He cannot put his finger on it.

Perhaps it is the sinister half-smile. Hardly surprising: he has won: he demanded Verhœven, he has been granted Verhœven, he defeated the experts, but even so, that smile . . . Given the state he is in . . .

Camille slams the door behind him, steps over to Jean, sits down and lays his hands flat on the desk.

"Let's not beat about the bush, Johnny Boy," he says. "You've got a scoop for me, that's what you told them, that's how you persuaded them to bring me back. Well

I'm here, I'm listening. You've got precisely seven seconds, one for every bomb, after that I leave this room, turn you over to my colleagues and go home to bed. One . . . two . . . three . . ."

He counts quickly.

"Four, five . . ."

He gets to his feet.

"Six . . ."

He takes a step back, preparing to leave.

"The bomb . . . the one in the school," Jean says.

Nothing about his voice betrays the weariness that is written all over his face.

"It's primed for this morning. Nine o'clock."

Camille dismisses from his mind the terrifying hill they have to scale in the next four hours.

"Yeah, you already told us that, it's hardly a revelation. I want something new, something hot off the press, otherwise I'm handing you back to the hit squad and . . ."

Jean cuts in.

"A kindergarten. I planted it in a kindergarten."

Camille grips his desk, the world is spinning.

"Which one, you little shit? Which school?"

Jean shrugs. I'm not saying another word.

A panicked Camille tries to remember how old kids are at nursery school, two, three, four? He has no children himself. A kindergarten . . . This is insane. There are more than three hundred of them in Paris. Just trying to imagine the victims, he feels physically sick. How could anyone do such a thing? Jean stares at the floor. Obviously, nothing matters except him, his mother, his demands, the whole world can drop dead, a hundred dead children seems a small price to pay for a ticket to Australia . . . Camille could happily kill the man. He could also try to reason with him, but that would be futile. Jean is stubborn, tight-lipped. In their earlier interviews, Camille tried to intimidate him, play on his fear, appeal to his compassion, his pity, he handed him over to the thugs from counter-terrorism, nothing has had the slightest effect.

"You know what I want," Jean says. "It's up to you. I get the impression you're not ready to deal, I don't know what more I can do . . ."

He shakes his head, apparently saddened.

"In the meantime," he says, "if you're going to need me, you'll need to let me get some sleep."

The handcuffs make it impossible for him to rest his head on his arms, so he bends down, lays his cheek on the desk and closes his eyes.

Immediately, his breathing slows.

He is asleep.

5.25 a.m.

Civil servants, engineers and specialists have been dragged from their beds, vehicles have been dispatched to collect them with outriders to clear the road, offices have been opened, computer systems booted up, all available data is being gathered. No matter how fast they work, every-thing takes time, it takes ages.

Over the past six months, work has been carried out

on almost every nursery school in the capital, the Public Services Department has to make the most of school holidays to do repairs. Any roadworks carried out in the neighbouring streets or in car parks adjoining the schools needs to be factored in. The most difficult thing to work out is the scale of the repairs: they need to focus on the jobs that took several days to complete and involved digging a trench large enough for Garnier to bury something the size of a mortar shell. One school was completely rewired, another had the toilet block replaced, they pore over blueprints, question engineers who frantically confer: would it be enough to plant a bomb or not? The pressure is hellish. One of the engineers breaks down.

"You can't ask that of me!"

He is worried sick, overwhelmed by the responsibility; someone drives him home and fetches his deputy. There are fifteen of them from a range of professions: road engineering, plumbing, excavation, roofing . . . Could you plant a bomb here? Here?

For the moment, they have not found any school, nor any road near a school where trenches were dug in the past eight months.

If you include all the possible hiding places for a mortar shell – sewers, cellars, basements, car parks – it quickly becomes a needle in a haystack.

"This school you mentioned, Jean, we can't find it . . ."

Jean looks up at the wall clock.

"You'll find it. It's just a matter of time."

He is not wrong.

Because fifteen minutes later, on the other side of Paris, in one of the decentralised offices of the *Préfecture de police*, someone picks up a telephone and angrily pounds his fist on the desk until it is finally answered:

"We've got it, we've found it."

As soon as the information reaches him, Camille races to the interview room, throws open the door, hurls himself at the suspect, grabbing him by the shoulders. A terrified Garnier tries to shield his face, but he is still handcuffed to the table.

"École Charles-Frécourt?" Camille roars. "Is that the one, Jean? Frécourt in the fourteenth arrondissement?"

Experts continue combing through their files, but the school on the rue Philibert-Beaulieu is the only possibility. Everything tallies. Three months ago, a sinkhole appears in the playground, a flustered headmistress calls the council, they call in surveyors and they in turn call in contractors, parents panic when they see a pit like a meteor crater, safety barriers are hurriedly erected, inspectors determine that the subsidence was caused by a leaking pipe that has weakened the substructure, the following weekend the schoolyard is dug up. In fact, it takes almost a week to shore up the damage, the children spend their playtime hanging off the safety barriers, twenty metres from the workers, as rapt as if it were a T.V. show.

Jean Garnier does not answer, he glares a Camille, then looks away.

5.40 a.m.

This time, there are no precautions, there is no time. As for the residents and the journalists, everything will be explained after the event. The most important thing is to get in there, find the bomb, defuse it; people check their watches as they race for the school. The police have cordoned off a section of the rue Philibert-Beaulieu, firefighters pull up right behind and lastly the hard-hat workers. The bomb disposal experts from *Securité civile* are already scanning the playground using ground-penetrating radar.

Basin has laid out the blueprints of the building on the ground, he barks orders while talking to Camille over the phone.

Things don't look as he had expected.

To Camille, this doubt is like a sucker punch.

"What do you mean by that?" he asks.

6.20 a.m.

"They've dug up the playground," Camille tells the *juge*, "but it was obvious as soon as they got there that it couldn't be the right school. The trench was too narrow for Garnier to have climbed down and planted the shell without anyone noticing."

A fact Jean has now confirmed.

"You didn't give me any time . . . I would have told you."

There are times when Camille wants to kill him.

The *juge* is now insistent that mother and son be

allowed to meet, and Camille no longer has any reason to refuse.

Rosie seems even more tense than she did earlier. Gaunt, emaciated. Her face a mask of utter dread. Camille takes a moment to study this woman, to ask himself the same question for the umpteenth time. What connection is there between the death of Jean's girlfriend and this wave of explosions?

What is the secret that binds mother and son?

The only way to find out is to bring them face to face. But though there are only three hours until the bomb goes off, Camille cannot reconcile himself to the idea. It is like standing on the brink of a bottomless pit and being forced to dive. Despite his better judgement, he takes the plunge.

"Your son is threatening to blow up a kindergarten, Madame Garnier! Do you have any idea what I'm saying?"

He explains. Even if they discover where the bomb is planted, they do not have enough time to make it safe.

Silence.

"But we would still have time to evacuate, do you understand? Otherwise, the bomb will go off with dozens of kids inside the school . . ."

Rosie nods. She understands.

"We need to know the location of the school, and we need to know right now!"

She is on the brink of tears, but she chokes them back, takes a deep breath. They have come to a closed door.

"He's in there?" she asks.

Camille opens the door. As soon as he sees his mother,

Jean bows his head. The officers standing guard step aside. Camille takes Rosie's elbow and leads her to the chair where she sits down heavily. Behind the one-way mirror and the monitors relaying the scene, thirty people hold their breath.

Rosie looks at her son. He stares at the wall above her head. Slowly, Rosie reaches forward, her hands sliding across the table in search of Jean's, two pale, lifeless creatures crawling across the cold polished steel that finally stop when Rosie, prostrate, can reach no further. Her face is pressed against the table, her arms extended in front of her, their hands are about twenty centimetres apart. It is almost unbearable, perhaps because of the silence and the time ticking away.

Rosie is sobbing, it is the only sound to be heard.

Jean is still stiff as a board, his face ashen, he does not move a muscle, does not look at his mother, he looks as though he has been lobotomised except for an involuntary quiver of the kind one sometimes sees in dogs, without knowing whether it is instinct or illness. The shudder that runs through Jean's whole body is mesmerising. Camille stares as two fat tears slide down Rosie's cheeks, sole witnesses to some intense emotion, some desperate loneliness.

Rosie lies across the table, Jean sits bolt-upright, the scene could play out for hours, days.

Camille is tempted to check his watch, but he cannot shake the idea that something extraordinary is happening here.

Because the expression on Rosie's face is not one of sadness. She squeezes her eyes shut, but not like a woman in pain. Is it the shock of seeing Jean again? Is it finding herself written into this story with him, with no way out? As he looks at her face, Camille has the strange impression he can see the child she once was.

Then, suddenly, it dawns on him.

This is not a look of sadness, or fear, or even of relief; it is a smile of victory.

Now Rosie lifts her head, her arms still stretched out before her, she makes no attempt to wipe away her tears, she stares at her son who continues to stare at the wall behind her head and she says, gently:

"I know you wouldn't abandon me."

Her voice is low, muffled.

"You can do it, I know you can ..."

As soon as he realises that it is a trap, Camille hurls himself at her.

"I love you, you know that."

Camille is already on her, gripping her shoulders, but she clutches the table. She screams.

"You're all I've got, Jean, you can't leave me!"

Camille pulls with all his strength, but what makes his blood run cold is Rosie Garnier's laugh, the feverish, manic laugh of a madwoman.

"I knew you'd come for me, Jean! I knew it!"

There is a general panic.

Louis is the first to emerge from the observation room. He bursts into the interview room followed by three other officers, together they seize Rosie, yet still she clings on, screaming "Don't leave me, Jean!" When they manage to relax her grip from the table, she clutches the chair, "You can't abandon me!", in vain they try to pull her away, her breathing is ragged with sobs, "They can't hurt us, Jean", and, when she refuses to let go, they are forced to drag her across the floor. She grabs the doorframe, they have to pry her fingers open, one by one, while her screams rise to a shriek. It is a pitiful spectacle.

Jean is still staring straight ahead.

He has not moved a muscle; it is impossible to know how he feels.

7.00 a.m.

Farida is a lovely woman, but she is very disorganised, everyone is fond of her, but honestly . . . She does a bit of work here, a bit of work there, drops everything and wanders off, you never know what she is up to. Usually, she starts work at 7.00 a.m., and on that point, she cannot be faulted: she is always punctual. But rather than concentrating on the classrooms as she has been told a thousand times, she starts by polishing the coffee machine, she dusts the headmistress' office, mops the floors in the staffroom and the corridor, then tackles the windows, moving from one job to another according to a logic no-one understands. The result is that, as staff and pupils arrive, she is all of a flutter, running round all over the place, but she is incorrigible; the next day, she will be just the same. She has been read the riot act a dozen times, but there is nothing to be done, this is just the way she is. The head teacher, Madame Garrivier, is frustrated. A week ago, she put Farida on notice: she telephoned the local council and asked for her to be reassigned. Not one to hold grudges, Farida said that she understood why she had been reassigned to the gym, something she doesn't like, the camphor and eucalyptus smell of Deep Heat, the tiled showers . . . She does not know it yet, but even if the head teacher had not put in the request, Farida would have been reassigned to the shower block since, a few hours from now, there will be no cleaning to be done, since there will be no school. It will have vanished into thin air. Knowing this, it feels somehow pathetic to watch Farida polishing the little desks, the little sink where the toddlers wash their hands, the toilets that look as though they were built for the seven dwarves; given that it will soon be dust and rubble.

The 140-mm mortar shell is buried less than a metre below the hallway the classrooms open onto. It is in a cellar that no-one ever visits since it is useless as storage, the roof is too low, but mostly it is prone to flooding, everything that can be done has been tried, but year in, year out it is frequently knee-deep in water. Ten years ago, when studying for his electrician's diploma, Jean did a placement at a company that did repair work on this school, he went down into this cellar many times. The company has long since folded, and Jean never became a certified electrician, having switched to studying electrical engineering, but he remembered this school. Because of the water, he had to create a plinth on which to set the mortar shell from breeze blocks and waterlogged hunks of timber that had been there for years. This was no bad thing, since it means the bomb is almost level with the floor of the corridor and the blast will meet with little resistance. The children file into the school at 8.15 a.m. Madame Garrivier is a stickler for punctuality. The bomb is set to go off at nine o'clock.

7.15 a.m.

They will have to resort to extreme measures, what other choice do they have? In the privacy of the president's office – surrounded by three ministers, the Chief of the Defence Staff and senior officials from the *Securité civile*, the police, etc. – veiled discussions were held in veiled terms, proposing gruesome ways to extort the truth from Jean Garnier.

As usual, there was talk of psychotropic drugs and truth serums, the stuff of dime-store novels, all of it quickly debunked by the experts: the way that subjects react is too unpredictable, their answers are often a jumble of truth and fiction, and in the time required to corroborate their statement, the bombs would probably explode.

Before they have finished explaining their theories, the president interrupts with a wave of his hand. He is a pragmatist; he would not balk at using unethical techniques, but it is too late for that.

"Time is on his side, *Monsieur le président*," someone tells him. "Threatening to set a bomb off every day, then surrendering to the police after the first explosion, was a very clever idea. Obviously, given the constraints, law enforcement agencies have done everything they—"

The president cuts the man off.

"Of course, of course . . ."

No-one knows what he really thinks, but they will find out before very long, because the carnage wreaked by this wave of terror will affect not only the schools and shops where Garnier has buried the bombs, but also the corridors of power. It is rare for an event of such magnitude not to cause collateral damage with an administration.

We have not yet reached that point.

The president picks up the report from the *ministre de l'Intérieur*. It is agonising to realise just how powerless he is. Scanning the report, the president nods, initiate the O.R.S.E.C. civil emergencies plan, yes, he has no choice, better safe than sorry . . .

He has to make a decision.

At 07:16 hours, the president gives the order to evacuate every kindergarten in Paris.

Every last one.

Three hundred and forty-nine schools. Forty-five thousand children.

Instantly, the military machine roars into life: shouted orders, footsteps echoing in the corridors, telephones ringing, people calling from one office to another. Guard patrols have to be organised, schools cordoned off, vehicles requisitioned, hundreds of soldiers dispatched, because it is not simply a matter of preventing people entering the schools, they have to have the resources to collect the children, ferry them to local sports halls, community centres, provide supplies and first-aid posts – it is a colossal undertaking. And they have less than two hours. It seems all but impossible but, within minutes of the president lighting the blue touchpaper, every branch of the military and the police force will be working at top speed. And they can do this.

But before that, there is something that is even more important than the evacuation: communication. This morning, Parisians will wake up to something akin to a state of war, fire engines and army trucks will be roaming the streets of the capital and they will be informed that their children are in danger from unexploded bombs . . . It is not difficult to imagine the reaction, in parliament, the opposition parties will be haranguing, demanding explanations. *Is the prime minister really saying that one man can hold the entire country to ransom? It beggars belief!* Precisely the sort of situation the prime minister relished when he was a member of the opposition: a government unable to ensure the safety of French children! A government caving in to the demands of a lone terrorist! Shameful! "The Government's abject cowardice is matched only by its utter incompetence!" – he savoured such slogans when he was still in opposition.

Now that he is prime minister, it is different.

He consults with his advisors, listens to his ministers, considers his personal position. He makes decisions. The prime minister will be first to speak, he will hold his fire until afterwards, when . . .

Then suddenly, things fall apart.

The O.R.S.E.C. plan is abandoned, crisis talks are called off, political statements are forgotten. Everything is cancelled because Camille Verhœven has telephoned, his message reaches the Élysée Palace at the speed of light.

Exactly four minutes ago, a pale, exhausted Garnier finally talked, his voice faint and hoarse, Camille was forced to lean close to hear what he was saying. Already dead on his feet, the confrontation with his mother has left him visibly shattered.

"The second bomb . . ."

Camille leaned closer, unable to decipher the words, something that made him feel queasy, like a torturer unable to understand the whimpering of his victim. At that moment, the mobile phone in his pocket vibrated. Camille muttered "shit!", contorting himself to remain in the same position while fishing his phone from his pocket: a text message from Anne: *Spent the night all on my own . . . very sad*. The contrast is shocking.

"Sorry, what?" Camille says, hearing the words "I am . . ."

Garnier whispers into his ear:

" . . . because I am a decent guy."

Camille recoils in shock.

"You're a decent guy? I have to say that's not the phrase that comes to mind . . ."

Garnier sways, almost falling from his chair, Camille leans towards him again.

"Don't bother looking," Garnier whispers. "The school . . ."

At last, something new, Camille stuffs the mobile into his pocket without replying. Garnier's bluff is finally yielding to the brutality of the situation. A shudder of relief courses through Camille right to his fingertips.

"What is it Jean? There's no bomb, is that what you're telling me?"

He grips the man's neck as he speaks.

"No, no . . . there is . . ." Jean mumbles. "But not in Paris."

And so everything is put on hold, the O.R.S.E.C. plan, the mass evacuations. The authorities reconsider their position.

The bomb is in a kindergarten somewhere in the provinces.

This is a catastrophe.

"Sixteen thousand nursery schools," announces the minister. "Two million children. It simply cannot be done."

They have considered the problem from every possible angle, but short of creating mass hysteria, there is no way to tell every head teacher in the country: "Some lunatic has planted a bomb in a school, it could be yours, we have no way of stopping him, so you all need to evacuate your schools and get as far away as possible."

Like the prime minister , the *ministre de l'Intérieur* is a pragmatist.

"Including parents, grandparents and relatives, we would have three million adults to deal with."

Especially since panic would spread to the population in general, since there would have to be a press statement explaining that this is merely the beginning, that there are five more bombs that cannot be located.

Nor is it possible to launch an inspection of every school, it would take months.

What makes it even worse is that no-one can be sure whether or not Garnier is telling the truth.

There is only one solution: wait for 9.00 a.m.

It is sickening.

Police officers, politicians, experts all slump into their chairs and contemplate the ability of modern democracies to withstand attack.

As Basin said to Camille: "People assume that terrorism is sophisticated. Actually, it's not."

8.15 a.m.
Lucas, Théo, Khalidja, Chloé, Océane and the other children hold hands and head down to the far end of the playground. It took weeks, no, months, to get funding from the local council, but Madame Garrivier is persistent. She dreamed of having a little vegetable garden, but good Lord, she had to plead, cajole, pester, just for a lorry-load of topsoil and a few stones! Now, finally, she has achieved her goal. A few months ago, the little plot was prepared. The children planted tomatoes, runner beans, flowers, they love working here. As does Mme Garrivier: her father was a farmer.

The children are four years old. On average. Because Maxime is barely three, while Sarah is about to turn five.

The school has six classrooms.

A total of one hundred and thirty-four pupils. But Mme Garrivier's class – twenty-two pupils – are the ones most directly concerned, because their classroom is right above the spot where Jean planted the bomb. This is not to say that others will not be affected, but this will bear the brunt of the damage.

In fact, the classroom will literally disintegrate. It will take no more than a second or two. There will be a neat hole in the ceiling, as though a cannonball was fired, as the supporting walls are rocked by the force of the blast, a whole section of the roof, like a huge black bird, will take wing, glide a short distance and crash into the vegetable garden.

Fire will take hold and, in less than an hour, the whole building will be reduced to ashes.

Jean set the bomb to go off at 9.00 a.m. precisely. From his point of view, it was a wise decision, since at that moment, all the pupils will be in class, except Madame Garrivier's, who are working in the vegetable garden.

8.30 a.m.
Camille stares at Jean. He is torn between bitterness, rage, violence, but it is all futile.

The young man is shattered, he has not had a moment's respite, he will not say anything, he will stand his ground. Camille knows this; he has stood his ground against the "experts". Even the duty psychologist is reduced to spouting platitudes. Camille has quickly skimmed the profile written by an expert who spent an hour with Jean, who did not utter a word: anxious, introverted, shows good emotional control. Fat lot of help that is, thought Camille.

"There's one thing I find surprising," Camille says. "In your case file, it says that you used to babysit for people on the estate. Several people mentioned this. They say you were a natural with kids. The parents were thrilled. They all said so."

Jean warily raises an eyebrow.

"I'm serious," Camille says. "You don't fit the profile of someone who plants bombs in nursery schools."

A shadow flickers across Jean's face.

"Are you a child murderer, Jean?"

Jean swallows hard.

"You'll see . . ."

8.53 a.m.

The past hour has felt like the calm before the storm. Not that people are idle, the police and the military continue to work furiously, like a losing football team refusing to surrender, battling on until the final whistle blows. Officers are still combing through Jean Garnier's past, trying to identify the school where he planted the bomb. The main problem is that local councils do not inform all and sundry every time they authorise repair works on buildings in their district. There is no central database, so they make do as best they can, telephoning municipal offices in major cities, sending emails and faxes that are greeted with sublime indifference, since they can hardly use the subject line: *Please reply A.S.A.P., there might be a bomb in your local school.* That would simply trigger panic and terror. To the bureaucrats receiving these emails, it hardly seems urgent to advise the ministry about public works carried out a month, three months ago, so they leave it until next week.

Time ticks on.

In the vast halls of the ministries, in opulent offices overlooking lush gardens, beneath the gilded pomp of the Republic, people hold their breath. Every possible scenario has been envisaged, but with only minutes to go, whether police officer or president, minister or civil servant, picturing a bomb devastating a hundred four-year-olds is harrowing and heartrending.

As the hour strikes, an eerie silence reigns; they feel as soldiers do before the order to charge: the urge to attack, to be done with this, even if it means death. Yet nine o'clock passes, nine-fifteen: nothing, Jean is still shackled to his table.

Camille has gone back to his office. Feverishly he rereads the case file, Louis' notes, scribbling over everything in reach.

9.21 a.m.

Offices begin to bustle once again, no-one dares to entertain a feeling of relief, time continues to tick away. Camille is still poring over the case file. The half hour strikes, the minister's office has been informed, the *préfet* has telephoned twice, the *juge* is pacing up and down like a first-time father outside the delivery room. Finally, they accept it: blessed relief, like Armistice Day.

Jean, for his part, is sweating.

His eyes, which were fixed, staring, now dart from the table to the door. Something has gone wrong.

Camille arrives and smiles.

"So tell me, Johnny, this day of reckoning, was it meant to be today or tomorrow?"

Beads of sweat run from Jean's eyelids, nervously he tries to wipe them away. He simply says "I don't understand . . ." He seems distraught, though as Camille studies him, he cannot quite describe what he is seeing. A curious mixture of confusion and detachment.

This bomb has not gone off. It does not mean that there are no others, but everyone agrees that this time, at least, the danger has passed.

Badin thinks it was probably a defective shell.

Everyone is now searching for the next bomb.

The interrogation begins again, the countdown is reset to twenty-four hours.

If there really is another bomb.

Blackmail or genuine threat? This is the real question.

"And it's also the trap," says Camille. "We end up chasing round looking for bombs that we know are statistically unlikely to explode . . ."

He is right. It is paradoxical, but Jean's threat is all the more effective because of this uncertainty: the authorities are left with the choice of haring around searching for bombs they have a vanishingly small chance of finding, or of doing nothing, of waiting and succumbing to the fear that one of them will explode, causing terrible loss of life, and they will not have lifted a finger.

There are two schools of thought.

Those who believe that Jean Garnier planted one shell in order to make his threat seem credible and that there is no longer anything to fear. And those who cannot decide, who vacillate and change their minds from moment to moment, who would like to be certain, but cannot be.

Between these two camps, or rather outside them, are Camille and Louis.

10.00 a.m.

Marcel, the park warden, is opening the iron gates of square Dupeyroux. He always checks his watch beforehand. In a petty act of rebellion for being a lowly council worker, he takes great satisfaction in opening a minute or two late every day. The lock on the gates is broken and, though Marcel has filled out the requisition and maintenance forms, it is useless, the maintenance crew refuse to show up. So at night, when he closes the gates, he simply uses a piece of cardboard to wedge them shut. No-one has noticed yet. It would be safer to get the lock repaired, because if the drug dealers notice, the park will be swarming after dark, the local residents will protest, the council will get in a lather and he will get it in the neck.

By the time Marcel completes his first tour of inspection, there are already people sitting on the benches.

He glances at a thicket of shrubs. Some weeks ago, he

noticed a hole where someone has been crawling through, he checked the area but found nothing, no syringes (he has nightmares about needles because of the children). Nothing but the steel hatch that leads down to the substation. Time was, he went down once or twice a month, for eleven years he dutifully checked and never found anything. Eventually he got bored, and besides, these days he suffers from arthritis and crippling back pain, so he has no desire to clamber down and scout around bent double, thank you very much. In any case, city maintenance crews check it three or four times a year. If there were anything to see, they would find it.

Marcel turns abruptly. He has "eyes in the back of his head", or at least, this is what he tells the children so they will be afraid of him. If someone steps on the grass, he may not see it, but he senses it. This time, it is a little girl. Marcel draws his whistle at lightning speed, the girl freezes, rooted to the spot.

10.15 a.m.
Without even realising, Camille has found himself outside the loop.

Jean Garnier has been handed back to the interrogation team; Camille does not expect anything will come of it.

"The Garnier case is mostly about the Rosie Garnier case," he said to Louis.

Louis thought for a fraction of a second and then agreed.

Since the early hours, they have been going through

everything about the case with a fine-tooth comb, interview records, dates and times, but they have focussed most of their energies on Rosie's file, because she is the key to this whole affair. Not that she was the mastermind behind her son's plans (they are too sophisticated, she would never be capable), but Camille cannot quite accept that she is simply Carole's murderer. Certainly, Rosie fits the profile of an impulse killer, someone who acts unthinkingly. That night, in a fit of anger, she took the car and lay in wait for hours, her fury steadily mounting, so that, the moment she saw Carole, the red mist descended: she mowed her down and drove off. She was so irrational that it did not even occur to her to leave the car anywhere but in her own lock-up.

This was the official version of events.

The entire case rested on this single unintentional oversight. The investigating magistrate was overwhelmed by his caseload, the detectives were satisfied they had Rosie Garnier in custody: everyone accepted this account. In fact, it will form the basis of the defence argument by her lawyer, Maître Depremont, a striking female barrister with a faint accent (German? Dutch?), capable of turning anyone to jelly. Camille looks at her hand, her wedding ring, he assumes she married a Frenchman. A perfect oval face, high cheekbones, eyes of a green seen nowhere else in nature. The moment she looks at you, you are lost. Camille telephoned her last night and asked her to come in for a chat. It was three o'clock in the morning, but she looked absolutely flawless. The interview did not last long, she had nothing much to say: as far as she was concerned the murder committed by Rosie Garnier was an instinctive act, she is planning to plead diminished responsibility. Which is certainly true, though perhaps not the whole story.

"Alright, thank you, *maître*," Camille said, not even troubling to ask any questions.

"I don't think she knows much," he said to Louis later. "And there's no point trying to probe any deeper, she'll just claim duty of confidentiality and all that shit. It was a complete waste of time."

Louis has been spending his time trawling the internet, printing out dozens of pages for Camille to read.

Housing: Rosie is scrupulous in paying her rent, she has comprehensive insurance, the apartment is a testament to her obsession with cleanliness.

Bank statements: Rosie does not earn much, yet she has modest savings – not much, but she saves.

Social security: Rosie is in rude health, rarely takes sick leave and is not taking any medication.

Local authority: she has repeatedly applied for social housing, her requests have always been declined, but she is not discouraged, she simply fills in another form. She has never applied for benefits – she suffers from the futile pride of modest people.

Employment history: in her time with her current employer, she has never been promoted and will likely remain at the bottom of the ladder until retirement, she does not apply for internal vacancies, has never requested a transfer, she is stubbornly deskbound. Has no ambition ...

11.00 a.m.

Like a teenager caught doing something wrong, Rosie lowers her head and screws up her mouth. She looks as though she has been caught shoplifting a T-shirt in a department store rather than encouraging her son to set off six bombs in Paris.

"So, tell me Rosie, little Johnny seems to be pretty traumatised by this whole 'father unknown' thing."

She cocks her head and gives Camille a glassy stare. Her mouth drops open.

"Oh, no!" Camille bellows into her face. "Don't give me any of that simpering shit. It might work on Jean, but you're dealing with the police now, Rosie. And we want the truth, am I making myself clear?"

Camille has a list of the objects retrieved from the cardboard suitcase found in her bedroom wardrobe: magazines from the 1980s, *Podium, OK Magazine, Top 50*, singles by power-pop duo Peter et Sloan, and Eurovision winner Marie Myriam, and a mind-boggling collection of pictures of the singer Joe Dassin. The autographed photograph dedicated to Rosie was pasted to the cardboard cover and ringed by heart-shaped stickers.

"Don't tell me then," Camille says. "I'll tell you: you were fifteen and you were knocked up."

At this point Rosie makes a mistake of the kind one should never make with an interrogator like Verhœven:

"They never got along, my father and him," she says, looking hurt. "My father was dead set against the marriage. When I say him, I mean Jean's father, and he wanted to get married, he really did, he even suggested we elope, but you have to understand, I couldn't leave my father, I just couldn't. He was all on his own after my mother died..."

Camille sighs and his lips curl into a smile.

"Cut the crap, Rosie, you're wasting your breath."

He is calm, his arms folded, head tilted slightly to one side.

"That's a story you cooked up for Jean. A tragic melodrama with all the stock characters: a strict father, a dead mother, an adoring boyfriend and, to cap it all, a love child. Something straight out of a Harlequin romance, you didn't have to look very far. Let me tell you the real story: you probably don't even know the name of the guy you slept with."

Rosie instantly blushes.

"O.K., I'll make a bet with you: you always told Jean that his poor dear *papa* left to go to Australia, am I right?"

12.30 p.m.

His name is René René. Some parents are frankly cruel. His father was a customs officer, René always claimed that was why he was dumb. These days, he is pushing sixty, he's protected by the statute of limitations, but he's still a bitter, twisted man, like many sour-faced alcoholics, the sort of guy who mutters into his moustache.

In fact, when his colleague calls him "René! René, get over here, like, now!" René simply mutters "Yeah, yeah, yeah, no need to panic".

He slowly climbs down the metal ladder. Last week, he "earned his boots", the pair the company owes him, it's the law, they have to provide regulation-issue boots. René carefully writes down the date by which they should arrive, if they are even a day late, he kicks up a stink. He does the same for his overalls. As it happens, the pair they gave him pinch so hard he can only wonder whether they gave him a half-size too small. Either that or his feet have grown, which doesn't seem likely. He has tried everything, stuffing them with wet newspaper overnight, wearing them while sitting in front of the T.V., nothing has worked, they still hurt like hell.

Every rung of the ladder is sheer torture, and he's up and down them all bloody day. Retirement can't come soon enough.

But retirement is far from certain for René René because, as he arrives in the telecoms substation, he finds himself nose to nose with his co-worker who is staring in horror at a 140-mm mortar shell to which is taped a digital alarm clock, its blue numbers blinking with every second.

2.00 p.m.

Garnier's aim is immediately apparent to anyone. The shell was planted in a telecoms substation beneath 144, boulevard de Mulhouse. During the day, it is a busy street, but not a major thoroughfare, a 140-mm shell might leave three people dead, a low return on the effort invested.

At night, however, at about eight o'clock, there are seven or eight people per square metre, because 144, boulevard de Mulhouse is a multiplex cinema, and the manhole entrance to subterranean digital exchange is located exactly where cinemagoers queue for tickets; if you include collateral damage (the huge plate-glass windows will shatter, sending millions of glass slivers and aluminium shards flying at least fifteen metres in every direction), you are guaranteed more than fifteen fatalities, and, at a conservative estimate, sixty injured.

As soon as he arrives at the site, Basin registers that the bomb is set to go off in the evening. He checks his watch – no need to panic – and decides on a plan of action: the surrounding streets are cordoned off, everyone within a 100-metre radius is evacuated. As always in Paris, within minutes all traffic in the city grinds to a standstill.

Then the *Securité civile* gets to work. Not so much bomb disposal experts, as *artists*.

Everything went according to plan: the evacuation, the police cordon, the reassuring public statement, the media kept at a respectful distance, even the dishonest press release from the local *préfecture* which, though unimaginative (a break in a gas main), proves convincing.

But the real glory goes to the bomb disposal experts, led by Basin. His initial assessment proved correct, the bomb was set to detonate three days from now at 8.15 p.m. According to Garnier's logic, this was bomb number five.

"The ordnance wouldn't have exploded anyway," Basin tells Camille over the phone. "There was no charge left in the detonator, and the primer was defective."

This is the good news.

Which leaves only the bad news: at nine-thirty this morning, when the nursery school bomb failed to materialise, everyone breathed a sigh of relief and assumed that Garnier's threat was nothing but bluff.

They now have proof to the contrary.

The first shell exploded on the rue Joseph-Merlin, the second failed to discharge, the fifth has been found and deactivated, this means there are still four out there.

One of which is set for some point in the next twenty-four hours.

6.00 p.m.

Camille went for an hour's sleep – an area of the canteen has been set up with cot beds where officers can take a short nap before heading back to their offices, eyes puffy with sleep, their faces drawn as one sleepless night drags on to the next. Camille lay down and immediately dozed off, but his sleep was anything but restful. His head is spinning with all the information he has gleaned from the files on the Garniers, transcripts of interviews, names, photographs, diagrams of mortar shells, even the image of the bewildered little boy with his empty clarinet case, lying on the rue Joseph-Merlin.

Once back in his office, he taps Louis on the shoulder, they swap places, and Louis goes for a rest.

While Commandant Verhœven was asleep, he created and printed a timeline of dates and events split into two columns: Rosie on the right, Jean on the left. They are looking for links, but they do not know what sort. Camille skims the first page, then the second. As ever, Louis' work is detailed and meticulous, nothing escapes him and, without seeming to, he works at extraordinary speed.

Page three. Page four. Page five.

Camille stops, flicks back, runs a finger under one line.

May, five years ago. Rosie Garnier is ill.

In the left-hand column, it is clear that during this period, Jean was not in Paris, he was in the Pyrénées-Atlantiques.

Camille is suddenly wide awake.

He gets up and searches for a report in a pile of papers on Louis' desk, but cannot find it.

"What are you looking for?"

He turns. It is Louis. He couldn't sleep and decided to come straight back. Without a flicker of hesitation, he locates the report concerning Alberto Ferreira, for whom Jean was working five years ago. Ferreira has since died. They look up the date: May 24. Louis does a quick internet search: May 24 was a Tuesday.

Camille has already found a transcript of the interview with Marie-Christine Hamrouche, Rosie's colleague and friend.

"[…] Rosie was always complaining about her son […] They were always at each other's throats […] when he talked about moving away, Rosie was delighted. You'd think she was the one who'd had a wedding proposal."

Finally, here it is:

Extract from witness statement

M.-C. Hamrouche: It was always the same. He'd go away, Rosie would come alive, then he'd come back and the fighting would start up again. It was non-stop.

Officer: Did Jean Garnier regularly spend time away from his mother's home?

M.-C. Hamrouche: No, not "regularly". Three or four times maybe. I remember four or five years back, he was working with a builder who moved down south to work and suggested Jean go with him. Because he was a good worker, that lad. Well, when he actually worked . . . Anyway. Rosie was so happy that she decided to take a holiday. It was very sudden, I guess it was the relief, more than anything. She talked to me that night, she was planning to set off the next day – and she was never one to travel. She went and spent a week with her aunt in Brittany.

Officer: And when did Jean Garnier come back?

M.-C. Hamrouche: He was hardly gone and he was back! Though it wasn't his fault, not that time, his boss was killed on a building site. So the whole thing about moving to the south wasn't going to work out, obviously.

[. . .]

The rest of the interview is of no interest.

Camille and Louis exchange a look.

If their hunch can be substantiated, they finally have a thread.

It will need to be unravelled, and that will take time, but it is the first glimmer of sunlight in a sky that has been overcast for days.

8.00 p.m.

Checks and cross-checks, corroborating evidence, supplementary questions, tests . . . Camille was reluctant to request outside help. Louis was not convinced, he pleaded his case, we're wasting valuable time, but Camille said:

"Until I'm absolutely certain, we tell no-one about this . . . I don't mind people thinking I'm a pain in the arse, but I don't want them to think I'm an idiot."

The observation room behind the one-way mirror is full: the *juge*, a couple of brass hats from the police, another from the *Préfecture*, and the Other who has just returned from the ministry . . .

In the interview room, Camille and Louis sit facing Jean Garnier, the former is empty-handed, the latter has a pile of seemingly innocuous papers.

"I don't know about you, Jean, but I'm starting to feel like we've known each other all our lives. I know you've barely been here twenty-four hours, but so much has happened in that time . . ."

Now freed from the handcuffs, Jean slowly rubs his chafed wrists. He has spent hours sitting here and must be aching to stand up, but he does not show it. He simply stares down at the table in front of him, utterly emotionless.

His eyes are red-rimmed, his face ash grey beneath the stubble that looks blue in the harsh fluorescent light. Perhaps the failure of his shells to detonate is taking its toll.

"We're pretty close, now, don't you think?" Camille says. "Thing is . . . you think you know someone and it turns out you don't know them at all. Take your mother for example."

Jean flinches. Ever since his arrest, his response to questions about himself, about what he did, where he went, has been to stonewall, but now that they are talking about his mother, a flicker of apprehension comes into his eyes.

"You look at Rosie, you think butter wouldn't melt in her mouth, and yet . . ."

Camille glances around as though making sure they are not overheard, then leans towards Jean to confide a secret.

"I don't think this is the first time she's been a bad girl . . ."

From Jean's reaction, Camille knows that his intuition has not failed him.

Louis slides the case file across the table and Camille opens it.

"Alberto Ferreira. Ring any bells? Oh, come on now, you worked for him a few years ago. As an electrician. Is it coming back to you? Thing is, you seemed to get along pretty well, the two of you. He hired you in January and by April, he's already giving you bonuses. Not a fortune, I'll grant you, but with employers, it's the thought that counts. He's pleased with your work. I have to say, from what I know of your technical skills, you're pretty good. Diligent. I'd even say meticulous. Obviously, you had to rely on the mortar shells still being active, but to judge from how you went about things, you have excellent organisational skills. What was I saying? Oh yes, Alberto Ferreira. So, what do you say, Johnny? Didn't have much luck, did he? Dead before he even turned forty. Life's a bitch, isn't it? And such shame, because he had big plans didn't he? The south of France, sunshine, blue seas. He buys a company in Biarritz that sells air-conditioning systems, decides to move there come September, and he's so happy with your work that he takes you with him. To Biarritz! So what did you think of Biarritz, Johnny? I mean is it nice, is it easy to find a place to rent? I only ask because I can see from this (he taps a document) that he sent you on ahead to get the lay of the land. You must have liked the idea, because before you can say 'suntan lotion', you're stuffing your suitcases. I mean, Rosie's sweet and all, but she was cramping your style, wasn't she?"

Jean swallows. His eyes dart round the room, vainly trying to anchor himself.

"So, there you are in the south of France, doing a bit of work, waiting for your boss, who's planning to show up a month later, when he's shut up shop and packed his belongings – and then, a week before he's due to leave Paris, one night when he's doing some last jobs on a site in the suburbs of Paris, Ferreira takes one step too many and falls head-first from the seventh floor. Goodbye Biarritz and air conditioning. The prodigal son heads home with his tail between his legs. Because you went straight back to *maman*, didn't you? Am I right so far? Well, the thing is, I found this story very moving. No, honestly, I swear, the enterprising entrepreneur, his hard-working electrician, it's inspirational. So, I took an interest. And, it's amazing what you find if you do a little digging . . . Coincidence can be fascinating . . . For example, did you know that when Alberto accidentally defenestrated himself, Rosie was on leave from work? Yeah, I know, the link isn't immediately obvious, but wait, you'll see where I'm going with this. Just after you left for Biarritz – the day after in fact – Rosie doesn't show up for work. She tells her best friend she's going to stay with an aunt in Brittany, but the thing is, Rosie has no aunt in Brittany, she has no aunts at all. And she's obviously in one hell of a hurry, because seeing that it's too late to apply for holiday leave, she phones in sick. But as she has better things to do than go and visit a doctor, she doesn't provide a sick note. She disappears for four days as though she doesn't give a damn about the consequences. And in fact, when she comes back, she is given a written warning and docked four days' pay. It was on the third day that Alberto died . . . Then, an hour or so to get back to Paris, have a quick wash and . . . You don't look convinced. Here, let me show you . . ."

Camille riffles through the file, takes out a sheet of paper, turns it around so that Jean can read it, but Jean shies away, he keeps his head down, like a stubborn animal refusing to move.

"This is a summary of the investigation conducted after Alberto died. No-one could work out what happened. It was nine o'clock at night, the building site was deserted, the only person there was Ferreira, laying cables before the screed floors went down. He's working all hours because he's sick and tired of this, he wants it done and dusted, he wants to head off to Biarritz, that's hardly surprising. Now, Alberto is an experienced builder, he's not the kind to go right to the edge of the deck and tumble over the protection barrier. And what happens? He falls arse over tit and lands thirty metres below! It's completely baffling. There are serious doubts. But, well, there was no-one on site, no trace of evidence on the body, he had no known enemies, no money to leave . . . What do you expect? The police and the prosecution service rule it an accident. Brought about by exhaustion, overwork. So far, so normal. When they examine Alberto's mobile phone, they find four calls from Rosie. At the time, the detectives didn't see this as suspicious. They questioned your mother, she said she phoned to ask him about you and that, since Alberto never answered, she had to call several times. If she'd wanted to know where he was, get in touch, or arrange a meeting, she would have done the same thing. She was the last person to call Ferreira . . . funny, isn't it?"

Camille suddenly stops.

"You still don't look convinced, Johnny. I have to admit, it does sound like I'm splitting hairs, but . . ." (He claps his hands as though he has just worked out how to square the circle.) "Talking about hair . . . Now, you'll say this is just another coincidence, but let's talk about little Mademoiselle Bouffant."

Jean continues to stare at the table, but his eyes are hard and glassy. Camille, who does not seem overly concerned, sees in it the same stubbornness he saw in Rosie. Family resemblances are often depressing.

"I said Bouffant – that was in poor taste, sorry. Her name is Françoise Bouveret. When was it you first met her?" (Camille looks down at the case file, Louis runs his finger under a passage.) "Thank you, Louis . . . it was March four years ago."

Camille takes off his glasses and calmly sets them down in front of him.

"Now, I'm not one to criticise, Jean, but I think you really made Rosie's blood boil. Because your ladylove, Mademoiselle Bouveret, well, she wasn't quite old enough to be your mother – and we only get one mother, huh? – but really . . . thirty-eight? She was thirteen years older than you. It's not just the age difference, and I don't want to offend, but with that cheap, gaudy jewellery and that tarty make-up – I've seen the photos – she was hardly the sort of girl your mother dreamed of for her only child. But never mind. You fancy her, you're really into her, you need experience, nothing abnormal about that, and you're so besotted that, three months later, you're packing a bag and moving in with her. This undying love lasts two months. We know that from your mother's case file, we did a little cross-referencing, we dug out the paperwork.

I'll spare you the details, but I have to admit you weren't exactly lucky. There you are, living the dream, with Mademoiselle Bouveret teaching you things you never imagined in your wildest dreams, and then she goes and decides to use her hairdryer while she's in the bath. Surely by the age of thirty-eight she would know better? There is a curious detail – the apartment door wasn't locked. The police were a little worried, obviously, they wondered if there was something fishy going on. You had no motive, obviously, and besides, you had an alibi. You weren't there, there were eight co-workers ready to swear on a stack of Bibles that you were with them on the building site in Poitiers. And none of us gave Rosie a second thought. At the time, she wasn't in the frame. But that was an over-sight on our part, if you get my meaning. I can tell that you know what I'm getting at. We're going to go through the file again, point by point, we're going to reopen the case . . . but back when all this happened, what it meant for you, Johnny, was slinking back home to *maman*. Ferreira, Bouveret, Carole . . . I'm thinking maybe Rosie can be a little bit clingy, huh?"

The atmosphere is oppressive. Camille leaves a long silence. Behind the one-way glass, his colleagues can finally see what Camille is getting at. Mentally, they all have their fingers crossed.

"Your mother is on remand for the murder of Carole. To the cops, it looks like irresistible impulse, no-one thought to dig any deeper. It's not as though Rosie fits the profile of a serial killer, everyone is happy to believe it was a moment of madness. But seen in a different light, if you look at her motive, ask the right questions, rake through the past, it's not hard to piece things together. It's a bit like your mortar shells . . . all it takes is a little planning."

Camille smiles loftily.

"You leave, she panics, she drags you back home, she can't live without you. You try to leave, but you can't live without her either. You know what she has done to keep you there, you know her better than anyone, you never talk about it, but you know what it is that connects you, what binds you to each other, this pact of silence. At first, you dare not say anything. Later, things spiral out of control, and that's what brought Rosie to where she is today. So, ever the dutiful son, you've come to rescue *maman* . . ."

Camille falls silent, he and Jean both stare at the floor. What is there to say? Exhausted, Commandant Verhœven slips down from his chair. He studies Jean's hands for a moment, the hands that trembled like leaves in the presence of his mother.

"When all is said and done, you're a good son. And maybe Rosie scares you. Hellcats can be like that . . ."

Silence.

"But it's now or never, Jean. You've caused a lot of damage, but so far nothing irreparable, right now you don't have any deaths on your conscience. When the day comes, a decent lawyer will be able to play the jury like a violin with tales of an abusive mother, they'll think you're a victim, and they won't be entirely wrong. If you give up now, you can kill two birds with one stone. You will finally be free of Rosie – it's high time – and you won't get dragged down with her. You have been here for twenty-four hours. If the authorities had any intention of giving in to your demands, they would have done it by now. But they won't cave. And, with the case we are currently building against Rosie, she'll never be released. You have one last chance to get out of this. You meet with the *juge*, you make a deal, you tell us what we need to know, and you're back on track. Look at me, Jean."

Jean does not flicker an eyelash.

"Look at me, Jean."

Camille's voice is low, gentle.

Eventually, Jean looks at him.

"Rosie is batshit crazy, you know that, don't you? She will never be released, it's a losing battle. Think about yourself. You did everything you could for her, and that's good, anyone can understand, everyone *will* understand. But it's over now."

Jean nods. Camille ponders for a moment: act now or let this sink in. There is too much at stake, he has to act fast.

"Are you ready to talk to me, Jean?"

Jean shrugs. He is ready. He blinks nervously, as though there were a spotlight trained on his eyes.

"Good," Camille says. "That's the right decision."

Jean nods again. Camille sits down, takes out his pen, closes the case file, he will make notes on the cover.

"Where should we start, Jean? I'll let you decide."

"With the ransom."

Camille freezes. From where he is sitting, he thinks he can hear panicked gasps behind the one-way mirror.

Jean Garnier does not give them time to catch their breath.

"Yeah, the ransom. I said I'd be prepared to accept four million. But that was yesterday. Now it's five million or no deal."

8.56 p.m.

Camille is devastated by this setback. He cannot understand. How could he make so many mistakes, how could he have orchestrated such a fiasco? He can hardly believe it himself. Petrified with fear, he appears before the *juge* and the director of the *police judiciaire* for a debriefing.

They are all gathered in the incident room, but the Other, the man from the ministry, does not bother to wait, he is already out in the corridor, whispering into his mobile phone, reporting back to his superiors.

From this moment, every one of them will remember the sequence of events.

Those who checked the time will have clearer memories, because it was at precisely 9.07 p.m. that the telephone rang.

The *juge* gave an exasperated shrug.

Louis stepped forward, lifted the receiver, listened, replaced it and shot the *juge* a look that stopped him in mid-sentence, and announced:

"An explosion has just completely destroyed a kindergarten in Orléans."

9.00 p.m.

Just as he always opens a minute or two after the official time, Marcel would dearly like to close the park a minute or two early. But it is impossible. Sometimes it is lovers canoodling in a corner, and by the time they are ushered out, dragging their feet, it is three minutes past nine. Sometimes it is teenagers hanging around, or showing up with cans of beer, he has to lay down the law and by the time they leave it is 9.05 p.m. Sometimes it's worse than that. He has tried everything, announcing closing time fifteen, even twenty minutes early, but it makes no difference, when it comes to closing time, he is cursed.

Except tonight. Who knows why, but it is the first time since . . . the first time in ages because it is so long ago that he cannot remember. Incredulous, he makes a final check. It is not quite nine o'clock, and the little park is deserted, as it should be.

This is so astonishing, that it makes him a little uneasy. Could he have missed something?

Unable to stop himself, Marcel makes another round, but no, there is nobody.

By the time he finally closes the gate, wedging it shut with the piece of cardboard, it is 9.04 p.m.

9.40 p.m.

It is as though the blast could be heard as far away as Paris. Everywhere is in turmoil. The minister's office requests information, there are concerns about the media, about widespread panic, senior police officers meet in conclave.

There were no victims, but the school was literally blown to smithereens. Thankfully, it is late, the morning newspapers are putting their early editions to bed, but there is still a little time. And they will need it, because no-one knows what is happening.

The emergency services are on the scene, the *Securité civile* has already confirmed that the details of the explosion correspond to the blast on the rue Joseph-Merlin.

The police are baffled.

The experts believe that when setting the timer, Garnier confused 9 a.m. and 9 p.m.

As a hypothesis, it seems scarcely credible.

Camille asks Basin whether such a mistake is possible.

"Perfectly possible. After all, the guy is an amateur – we've seen stupider mistakes. Why do you think so many bombers wind up blowing themselves to kingdom come? Garnier is a dangerous man, but if he's also careless, then all bets are off. There are still four shells unaccounted for, but if he's been sloppy in setting them, even he can't help us."

In the frantic bustle and the cacophonous jangle of telephones, Louis glances over at Camille.

Moments ago, he was tense, now he seems relaxed, pensive, he looks as though he's about to go home after a hard day's work. He gets to his feet and, still calm and focussed, walks through the incident room, along the corridor, down two flights of stairs, takes a right turn, passes the uniformed officer outside the interview room where Jean is sitting, goes into the observation room next door.

He takes a seat, as though about to watch a movie.

Through the one-way mirror, he sees Pelletier from Counterterrorism working on Jean with two other officers. Standing with his back pressed to the wall, heels together, hands on his head, Jean's head sways as he struggles to keep his eyes open, looking as though he might collapse at any moment.

"You planning on killing more people?" Pelletier barks. "How many people are you prepared to kill to save that bitch of a mother of yours?"

"As many as it takes . . ."

Camille reaches over and turns off the sound. He concentrates on the image. The nursery school, the bomb set to explode at 9.00 p.m., it doesn't add up. The facts are there, but he scans Jean's face for something else, something he has missed until now. He feels heartened that his hunch about Rosie proved correct: maybe she is an impulse killer, but she seems to feel the impulse pretty frequently.

Until now, events have forced the police to think logically.

According to a logic imposed by Jean.

To find the solution, he needs to think outside the box. But how?

Camille spends almost an hour observing Garnier, watching his lips move, the officers come and go, the pressure mounting.

He breaks off for only a minute to read a text message from Anne: *Are you suddenly invisible or have we broken up and you forgot to tell me?*

11.00 p.m.

Camille takes Louis to one side.

"Routine maintenance visits to telecoms stations, are they scheduled in advance?"

"I'll have to look it up, but I think they operate on a three-monthly timetable . . ."

Louis does not ask why.

"Can you show me?" Camille nods towards the computer monitor.

DAY THREE

1.45 a.m.

"No," says the *juge* indignantly. This is also the response of the *commissaire divisionnaire*, but he knows Verhœven well enough to realise there is no point taking offence. "No," snaps the *préfet de police*, who seems unsurprised by the suggestion and treats it as an oddity, as though he has just been asked whether he wants salt in his coffee. There is no point even asking the officers from the counter-terrorism unit . . .

Louis pushes back his fringe, he was expecting this, as was Camille. The Other acted surprised and pretended not to understand.

"Release Jean Garnier? Are you winding me up?"

For the first time, he gives Louis a condescending look; it is always a relief to find a chink in a rival's armour.

"Any other suggestions? Maybe you think we should award him the *Légion d'honneur* while we're about it?"

And he gives a scornful snigger. Cheap jokes intended to humiliate are not things one should use against a man like Camille Verhœven.

"You're a moron."

The Other looked him up and down, but Camille does not give him time to react.

"You're a moron because you are incapable of understanding anything you cannot feel. You take everything Jean Garnier says literally because he seems naïve, but it is your logic that is flawed. You look at him but you don't see him. You don't understand him, you label him. Jean Garnier is a dangerous young man, but not because he has planted bombs. In fact, he has done everything in his power to ensure there is no loss of life, only material damage. But despite his best efforts, no-one can be sure that all of the mortar shells will prove to be relatively inoffensive. There are too many unknowns, too many unpredictable factors. On the rue Joseph-Merlin the scaffolding could have collapsed on a passer-by. In Orléans, the blast could have killed someone out walking their dog . . . Sooner or later, there will be a death toll. When you think about it, there is only one thing to do. If we release Jean and his mother, there will be no deaths. I guarantee it. If we keep them in custody, it's more than likely there will be carnage. It's up to you."

The Other is affronted, but he is also a professional.

In ministerial terms, a professional is someone who passes information up the chain. This nugget of information rises through the ranks. Then it comes back down again. The answer is still no.

"They don't believe me," Camille says.

It will take him twenty minutes to make his decision.

And thirty seconds to say to the *juge*: "O.K., it's all down to you now. If you have no objections, I'm heading home, I'm completely shattered."

2.10 a.m.

Paris is deserted, traffic is flowing freely. Camille takes advantage of a green light to fish his mobile phone from his pocket. At the next traffic light, he writes a text message to Anne: *Is the invitation for (the rest of) tonight still open?* At the third set of lights, he receives her reply: *The door has been open since last night.* Usually this is the last traffic light, but Camille is forced to pull over when he receives another message. It is from the *juge*: *Camille, you've been summoned to the Hotel Matignon to see the premier ministre, should I send an escort?*

– *Sorry darling, I've been summoned by the prime minister.*

– *That's the most pathetic excuse you've come up with.*

– *Sadly, it's true, I'm on my way there now.*

– *Are you spending the night with him?*

– *Probably not. Unless he asks – I can hardly refuse. He is the* premier ministre.

– *Can you ask him for a rent-controlled apartment for me? In the seventh arrondissement . . .*

– *O.K., but what do I do if he asks me to stay the night?*

– *If the apartment is in the fifth, the sixth or the seventh, let him have his wicked way with you. Anywhere else, and you come back here and fuck me instead.*

– *Deal.*

2.30 a.m.

The prime minister is not remotely sexy. They never are. If fact, it seems to be a criterion. But he is charming and polite, he gets to his feet, warmly shakes Camille by the hand ("A pleasure, *Commandant*"), gestures to a chair. There are eight or nine other people in the vast office. When Camille sits, everyone else takes a seat. *Monsieur le premier ministre* indicates the tape recorder on the coffee table.

"I have been made aware of your hypothesis, *Commandant*, but I would be grateful if you could talk me through it."

"Up until now – and despite appearances – Jean Garnier has done everything possible to ensure he did not kill anyone. The bomb on the rue Joseph-Merlin was planted after the scaffolding was erected, and he planted the shell where it would cause the minimum amount of damage. In Orléans, he only pretended that he had made a mistake, the bomb was deliberately set to go off when there was the least danger to human life. As for us finding bomb number five, this was not a happy accident: the maintenance schedule is freely available online. Garnier chose this particular telecoms station *knowing* there would be a routine visit yesterday, that we would find and disarm the device. From the start, his whole strategy has been to make us believe he is dangerous. So far, there have been three bombs. The first shocks us, the second terrifies us, the third sends us into a tailspin ... And that's as it should be, because we are sitting on a powder keg. He has planted seven devices, we have dealt with three, the rue Joseph-Merlin, the nursery school in Orléans, and the telecoms station beneath the cinema; there are four still out there.

We know they are set to go off sometime this week, and I'm betting that he has done his best to make sure there will be no loss of life, but even if I'm right, there is no way of knowing whether our luck will hold. We're completely at the mercy of his manipulations, the materials he's used and the accuracy of his calculations. He is organised and resourceful, but he's an amateur. And if he has made even a single mistake, we are the ones who will pay. Very dearly."

Camille hesitates for a moment, then drives the point home.

"Curious as it may seem, *Monsieur le premier ministre*, Jean Garnier is not a murderer."

Silence.

"But, by my calculations, he is about to become one in spite of himself. Sooner or later, something will go wrong with one of the four remaining bombs, it's inevitable. And there will be fatalities."

The prime minister puckers his lips to indicate that he understands.

"And when that happens, we'll only have ourselves to blame. Especially since he's given us a clear warning."

He leans forward and, without asking permission, presses a button on the tape recorder.

"*No* (the voice is that of Jean), *that's not the way it was . . .*"

Camille presses Fast Forward and then Play.

"*You're right about the first bombs,*" Jean says. "*I didn't want to have to kill anyone. But the last one, well, that's different . . .*"

"*Different how?*"

"*The thing is, if the last bomb explodes, then it means that I've failed. That this whole plan has been a fiasco. I'll have nothing to lose. So, for the last bomb, I've planned something . . . lethal.*"

Silence.

"*Something devastating . . . Please believe me,* Commandant, *you have to believe me.*"

Camille stops the tape.

"What are you proposing?" asks one of the suits – Camille does not know who he is.

"That we release them, him and his mother, in exchange for the location of the remaining devices. I don't think they'll go very far . . ."

Release them. The hostility is palpable. *Not very far*, what does that mean? Nine civil servants exchange sceptical glances; they cannot work out where Camille is going with this, what he is thinking. Camille has been waiting for this moment to plant the final nail.

"With the last shell, Garnier is planning to cause carnage. Maybe one of you here has some idea how we're going to explain the first two explosions to the press and the public, not to mention his grand finale, if not, you better start racking your brains, because it won't be easy."

"*Commandant.*" The prime minister gives him a sincere smile. "Could you give us a minute?"

Camille goes and sits in a vestibule four times the size of his whole apartment. He turns on his mobile phone. Message from Anne:

– So??? Am I getting my rent-controlled apartment?

– Too early to tell. He's in the bathroom freshening up . . .

– And you're sure it'll be in the seventh arrondissement???

– He says that will depend on my performance.

– I hope you're on form!

– Do you know what time it is???

– Same time as it is here, and I'm VERY up for it.

– I'll do my best and . . .

"*Commandant?*"

Camille looks up.

"*Monsieur le premier ministre* is ready for you . . ."

4.00 a.m.

"It's the best I could do, Jean. You give us the location of the bombs just before take-off. We can't wait until you land in Australia. That's the deal. If you don't like it, it will be out of my hands, you will have to talk to someone else."

Jean thinks for a long time, then says:

"No, three hours after take-off."

"That's not possible, Jean. You've got what you asked for, but you can't lay down all the conditions."

It takes them almost twenty minutes to come to an agreement. Jean will send the details just after the plane takes off.

"If we don't get the message, the plane will turn around and drop you back on the runway with your darling *maman*, is that clear?"

It is insane that Jean would agree to such conditions. That someone who has planned this mission with the skill of a master should fall into such an obvious trap. He puts up only a half-hearted protest.

"How do I know the plane won't turn back the moment I've sent the details?"

Since the beginning of this conversation, Camille's voice has grown hoarse. Though it sounds like weariness, in fact it is wretchedness. Just imagine. You are talking to a man doomed to die very soon, and you are expected to sound as though he has his whole life ahead of him . . .

"It's in no-one's interest for you to stay here . . ." Camille patiently explains. "If you do, we would have to arrest you, charge you and send you for trial. Which would mean explaining that we lied to the public and hushed up two explosions, that we did a deal with a piece of scum like you, handed over two million in cash, two tickets to Australia and false passports issued by the French government itself. We'd look like complete fucking idiots!"

Jean seems happy with this explanation. It is mind-boggling.

Everyone in the observation room is thinking "Dumb fuck!" It is an impression that experts often have of amateurs. They take them for fools.

It takes another hour to pretend to iron out numerous details which are of no importance and serve only to make the agreement seem credible.

In fact, as Pelletier tells Camille:

"Jean sends his message via the crew, details of the locations etc., we check them out . . . and we arrest him."

It is depressing in its simplicity.

Camille longs to ask Pelletier whether he is taking *him* for a fool, too. Because this is not how it is going to play out. The counterterrorist squad is not going to trouble with minor details, it is in no-one's interest for Jean Garnier to become a shitty stick with which to beat the government.

To say nothing of the fact that, if Jean were to hold off on sending the message for an hour after take-off, it would mean arresting him while in another country's airspace, and that would be complicated.

The experts claim they will have no trouble discreetly arresting Jean as soon as they get the green light. They have taken every precaution. Camille thinks it is more likely that a hit squad will be occupying the two seats behind Jean and his mother, and the two seats in front, with two or three others posing as cabin crew. If Jean keeps his end of the bargain, he will be quietly garrotted before the plane reaches the end of the runway. That, or something like it. Something discreet and deadly, something that acts within seconds. The same will happen to Rosie. And then the plane will brake as it taxies, and an ambulance will appear. So as not to create panic, the captain will make an announcement that the delay is due not to a mechanical fault, but to the sudden illness of two passengers. The cabin doors will be opened, the bodies will be deplaned and the plane will depart as though nothing had happened. None of the other passengers will know the truth, not that this matters; the authorities

133

simply need a way to get the bodies off the plane and onto the immaculate stretchers that have been previously prepared to the occasion.

At worst, if Jean does defer sending his message, they will revert to plan B. The plane will turn back; the air traffic lanes will have been reserved for the purpose.

We'll see, Camille thinks.

From the outset, nothing in this affair has gone according to the rules, he does not imagine for a second that it will end as expected.

In the meantime, he plans, organises, negotiates and, since the crisis team is made up of officers from various agencies, he fields advice from colleagues and takes orders from his superiors.

Jean did not inspect the suitcases, nor the clothes officers have fetched from his house.

"Do you want to check them?" Camille asks.

Jean is perfectly aware that tracking devices will have been planted among the clothing.

"It doesn't matter," he says, snapping the lid shut.

Nor does he take any interest in the money. Final negotiations settled on two million euros. A suitcase full of high-denomination banknotes should be enough to animate even the most jaded soul.

Lastly, he is given the passports. He flicks through them, nods his head.

He has become Pierre Mouton. Rosie's new name is Françoise Lemercier. Jean is not at all happy.

"Mouton is a ridiculous name."

Even Camille finds the idea of naming someone after a sheep before leading them to the slaughter pitiful.

"Take it or leave it."

Jean takes it.

Then he looks at the plane tickets.

"Can I check the reservations?"

He is ushered to a computer terminal. Camille expected him to be a computer whiz, but he is anything but, he types slowly and carefully.

He checks the flight number, confirms the reservations.

He looks relieved.

4.30 a.m.

Finally, Rosie arrives.

Her face is radiant, rested; she is a different woman.

As soon as she sees Jean, she throws herself into his arms, but the young man is like marble. Arms dangling limply by his sides, he stares into the middle distance. Rosie does not even notice, probably because she and Jean have finally been reunited.

When she steps back, he barely looks at her. They are left alone so that they can change for the flight. The C.C.T.V. camera shows them standing three metres apart, as though in different rooms. Jean frowns, intensely focussed on changing his clothes. Rosie shoots him admiring glances.

When the officers come back into the room, Rosie looks at them as if they are schoolboys who still have much to learn.

Camille hands Jean a mobile phone.

"You need to write the message *before* take-off," Camille reminds him, one last time. "It needs to be detailed, we need precise locations. All the remaining bombs are in Paris?"

"Yes."

"Good. The only number in the contacts list is mine. You can call me at any time before take-off for any reason, if you need to. I am your only contact, that's how you wanted it."

"Alright."

"O.K. The flight leaves for Sydney at 5.45 a.m. Is everything clear?"

Jean nods. Everything is clear.

In fact, it is pitiful.

He may have planted bombs, may have gambled with the lives of hundreds of innocent victims, but this young man playing a third-rate secret agent, his every move borrowed from a B-movie, is somehow touching. Perhaps it is his innocence. They all play out their roles, but everyone feels apprehensive; ever since Jean compromised on his demands, it has all felt too easy.

Camille, for his part, is still prepared for any eventuality.

While Jean and Rosie were dressing, he even made a bet with Louis.

"What do you mean?" Louis asked. "What else could possibly happen?"

Camille has no idea. Yet he is certain. It will play out differently.

"There will be something that we've overlooked . . ."

In mid-May, dawn has already begun to break by 4.30 a.m. Through the open window, Camille takes in a lungful of Paris air not yet poisoned with exhaust fumes.

Down below, he watches as Jean and Rosie leave, each carrying a suitcase.

Jean refuses to get into the waiting car, an officer rushes over, there is a heated discussion, but Jean will not be swayed, he hails a taxi. The officer stands there, helpless.

Camille closes his eyes, feeling overcome.

The taxi is one that the police laid on, the driver looks convincing.

Jean does not allow the driver to get out, he puts the cases in the boot, waves at Rosie to get in, the taxi pulls off.

Time to go.

Camille pulls on his jacket, goes downstairs and climbs into the back seat of car No. 1.

5.00 a.m.
Already the car is cracking with the voices from the pursuit vehicles.

"Target at eleven o' clock. Car 34, over to you . . ."

"Car 34 receiving. Target spotted at one o'clock."

The taxi carrying Jean and his mother moves through Paris followed by an invisible throng of some fifteen people in cars, vans, motorcycles . . .

It looks like a ghostly funeral cortège.

The microphone in the taxi picks up nothing but the silence of the passengers. Camille pictures Rosie snuggled against her son, feverishly clutching his hand and

Jean, indifferent, staring out the window as Paris flashes past . . .

On the G.P.S. monitor, Camille is studying the route taken by the taxi when he hears Jean's voice:

"Take a right here."

The driver pretends not to understand. A seasoned professional, he plays for time and misses the turning.

"That's not the way to the airport, *Monsieur* . . ."

"It doesn't matter," Jean says. "Take the next right."

His voice is clear and resolute. The driver puts on the indicator and turns onto the boulevard.

"Car 34, target heading west."

"Received. Over."

The voices of the pursuers are not yet flustered, but something is amiss.

Camille feels a brief shudder down his spine and realises: the time has come.

Almost.

Not yet, but almost.

Evidently, this is not the way to the airport. Has Jean got one last ace up his sleeve? It is perfectly possible.

"Target sighted bearing north, north-east."

"Target turning onto rue Plantagenet."

Target here, there and everywhere, Camille thinks. We're about to find out just how well the experts' scenario plays out.

5.15 a.m.

At Jean's instructions, the taxi takes another right and is now heading due south, directly away from Charles de Gaulle airport.

Over the crackle of the speakers, voices are raised, what the fuck is he doing, this arsehole. Camille's mobile rings every twenty seconds. He turns it off. Shit.

He is as tense as everyone else.

Are they being taken for a ride?

Through his driver's earpiece, the various teams ask Camille for instructions.

"Maintain pursuit, hold back, wait and see."

Still the taxi keeps turning this way and that. They can hear Jean's voice giving the orders.

The driver pretends to be irritated:

"Where the devil are we going? You're going to miss your plane, *Monsieur . . .*"

This is the designated code for requesting instructions. Camille does not even profess to have the situation under control, the reality is that they are going along for the ride, what else can they do?

Jean clearly knows where he is going, which is what has everyone worried.

He knows, and we don't.

Finally, the taxi pulls up outside the gates of the square Dupeyroux, a small park enclosed by elegant Haussmann buildings. The streetlights on the roads that ring the square give off a soft blue-yellow glow. The car carrying Camille drives straight past the taxi, takes a right and screeches to a halt. Everyone is waiting for instructions. All units are on standby. Their timing is shot to fuck.

Jean's voice:

"Wait for us here," he tells the driver.

The bodycam of one of the outriders captures Rosie and Jean as they get out of the taxi. On the monitor, they can be seen standing in front of the gates, a radio microphone hidden in the folds of Rosie's coat picks up her tremulous voice.

"Why did we come here, Jean?"

His response is inaudible, if indeed he does respond.

Jean pulls the gate, which slides open noiselessly. Marcel's wedge of cardboard falls to the ground. Jean does not bother to pick it up, though he has done so many times in the past.

Camille leaps from his car and begins to run.

In seconds, he has reached the gate, shouting to all units to stand down, the die is cast, how many bombs are going to explode? Where and when?

Already, Rosie and Jean are moving through the shadowy park, bathed in an orange glimmer. Just as Camille enters the square, they stop near the children's playground. Jean drops Rosie's hand, takes a few steps and disappears for a moment.

Seconds pass with the glacial slowness of a ticking time bomb. Camille considers making a lunge, but does not have a chance before Jean re-emerges from a thicket holding a mobile phone. He turns to look at Camille.

It is a strange, suspended scene.

In the faint glow of the square, Rosie stands, gripping her old lady's handbag; next to her, her son Jean, holding his phone, and lastly there is Camille, rooted to the spot, wondering what is about to happen.

Jean looks down at the phone and almost immediately tinny music begins to play. He turns up the sound.

Camille strains to hear, he watches as Jean holds out his hand, palm up, as though he is inviting Rosie to dance; and that is what it is, a dance, Jean and Rosie in each other's arms.

They are waltzing. She is gazing at him like a lover, he is still staring into space, but hugs her to him hard, very hard . . . Hardly have they whirled three times when Jean, still keeping time, slips a hand into his jacket pocket.

Suddenly, Camille recognises the song, "Rosy and John", a golden oldie from the sixties by Gilbert Bécaud.

We loved each other like no-one ever
Rosy and John, we were good together,
But life, is life, oh, but life . . .

As he twirls her, Jean stands facing Camille. He stands head and shoulders over his mother, who looks as slight and frail as a little girl. He looks steadily at Camille, who feels his mobile vibrate in his pocket.

He whips it out quickly.

It is a text message from Jean.

There are no more bombs. Thank you for everything.

Camille looks up. Something Basin said comes back to him.

141

". . . anything capable of producing an electrical pulse could be used as a detonator: a doorbell, a mobile phone . . ."

Camille is about to throw himself to the ground when the bomb explodes beneath the dancers' feet.

The force of the blast catches him right in the stomach, propelling him backwards, where he rolls over and over on the dirt path.

The boom is loud enough to make your eyes start from your head. Windows around the square are shattered, and there comes an ear-splitting crash of broken glass. The playground has disappeared, all that remains is a crater three metres wide and one metre deep.

Louis comes running and rushes over to Camille.

Sprawled on the path, his face covered in blood, one cheek pressed against the dirt, he has the bewildered expression of a little boy.

A few metres from Camille and Louis, the trees in the square have begun to blaze.

PIERRE LEMAITRE was born in Paris in 1951. He was awarded the Crime Writers' Association International Dagger, alongside Fred Vargas, for *Alex*, and was sole winner for *Camille*, *The Great Swindle* and *Blood Wedding*. In 2013, *The Great Swindle* won the Prix Goncourt, France's leading literary award.

FRANK WYNNE is an award-winning translator from French and Spanish. His previous translations include works by Virginie Despentes, Patrick Modiano, Javier Cercas and Michel Houellebecq.